'I have only one question that needs an answer. Do *you* want to be my wife?'

Eyes lowering, Ione trembled, compressed her lips, then parted them again. An obvious question, one that she should have foreseen, but harder to answer than she could ever have dreamt, for by nature she was not a liar. And when she lifted her lashes and collided with the dark golden intensity of Alexio's questioning gaze, her breath feathered in her throat.

Sentenced to stillness by the sheer mesmeric effect of his beautiful eyes, Ione murmured, half under her breath and without really knowing where the words had come from, 'I want to marry you more than anything else in the world.'

Lynne Graham was born in Northern Ireland and has been a keen Mills and Boon® reader since her teens. She is very happily married, with an understanding husband who has learned to cook since she started to write! Her five children keep her on her toes. She has a very large dog, which knocks everything over, and a smaller Highland Terrier. When time allows, Lynne is a keen gardener.

Recent titles by the same author:

THE ITALIAN'S WIFE
AN ARABIAN MARRIAGE
THE DISOBEDIENT MISTRESS

THE HEIRESS BRIDE

BY
LYNNE GRAHAM

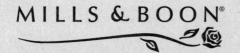

MILLS & BOON®

MILLS & BOON and MILLS & BOON with the Rose Device are registered trademarks of the publisher.

First published in Great Britain 2002
Harlequin Mills & Boon Limited,
Eton House, 18-24 Paradise Road, Richmond, Surrey TW9 1SR

© Lynne Graham 2002

ISBN 0 263 82961 8

Set in Times Roman 10½ on 12 pt.
01-0902-53454

Printed and bound in Spain
by Litografia Rosés, S.A., Barcelona

CHAPTER ONE

'SOONER or later, you will surely choose to marry *some-one*,' Sander Christoulakis pointed out, his emphasis of that last word reluctant. 'Why not Ione Gakis?'

Alexio made no response. On one level, he could not believe that this peculiar conversation was actually taking place. Once he would have laughed in his father's face at the very idea of an arranged marriage. But, for almost two years, Alexio had been living in a hell of grief from which he only escaped when he buried himself in work. In a desperate attempt to obliterate the yawning emptiness inside him, he had flung himself into a series of wild affairs but no miracle recovery had followed. Indeed, if anything, those shallow sexual entanglements had left him with a sour taste in his mouth.

'It is an honour that Minos Gakis should have approached our family with the offer of his daughter,' Sander continued with quiet persistence, watching his volatile son with hopeful measuring eyes for his reaction. 'He has a very high regard for your business acumen and his health has been troubling him. He *needs* a son-in-law whom he can trust.'

Alexio was grimly amused by that clever speech, which suggested that a marriage arranged between families rather than by the young people concerned was as common an event as it had once been in Greece—for it was anything but. He was also marvelling at how the attention of one of the world's richest men appeared to have blinded his astute father to less palatable truths. 'Minos Gakis is an evil bastard and a thug. You know it and I know it.'

'Nevertheless, his daughter, Ione, *is* a well brought-up and decent young woman,' Sander continued with determination, convinced that only such a marriage would have the power to remove his son from the partying, headline-grabbing lifestyle that was currently breaking his adoring mother's heart. 'I see no reason why—given time—you shouldn't find happiness with her.'

No reason? Bitterness hardened Alexio's lean, powerful face, his brilliant eyes darkening. He could no longer imagine being happy with any woman. But Crystal, the woman he had loved beyond any other, was undeniably *gone*. But then the issue of his late fiancée was not a subject his father would care to tackle, for the older man was no hypocrite.

Alexio's conservative Greek parents had hated Crystal and had refused to accept her as a bride for their only son. Her wild-child reputation and chequered past had offended their sensibilities. When he had put an engagement ring on her finger, his father had been outraged and his mother had wept, and for months afterwards Alexio had cut his parents out of his life. Only in the wake of Crystal's death had the divisions begun to heal and, even then, only because he had initially been in such a haze of despair that he had been incapable of rousing himself to the effort of rejecting his family.

Yet since then every business deal he had touched had turned to solid gold. He was now infinitely richer than his father had ever been for, while Sander had inherited his shipping fortune and merely conserved it, Alexio had gone into venture capital and software development, taking risks that his more cautious father would never have countenanced. It was ironic that only his own massive monetary gains in recent months could have put him in a position where the billionaire tycoon, Minos Gakis, would consider him as a potential son-in-law.

'I have never even met Gakis's daughter,' Alexio said drily.

'You *have*,' Sander contradicted immediately, his brows pleating. 'According to Minos, you met her when you spent the night on Lexos.'

In his turn, Alexio frowned, but even more darkly. A couple of months back, his yacht had run into difficulty in rough seas off the coast of the island of Lexos and he had radioed for permission to dock there, for Gakis was notorious for the brute henchmen he employed to guard his private island from unwelcome visitors. As it had transpired, Alexio had been made very welcome, indeed lavishly entertained by the reclusive tycoon, but it had been an evening almost surreal in its ghastliness.

Although he was well into his sixties, Minos had had a mini harem of beautiful bimbos staying in his palatial villa and Alexio had been invited to choose one of those women to complete his night's entertainment. He had been revolted by how very willing the fawning females involved had been to satisfy the older man's jaded tastes. Even so, Alexio had not made the dangerous mistake of discussing Minos's proclivities with anyone on his return home. Minos Gakis would make an implacable enemy and only a fool would risk awakening the ruthless older man's wrath to no good purpose by talking out of turn. And when it came to anything that might threaten his thriving business empire, Alexio Christoulakis was no fool…

Surely one of those bimbos could not have been Ione Gakis? Beneath his father's bewildered scrutiny, Alexio vented a humourless laugh at that unlikelihood for, though Gakis was far from being a likeable character, he was not unhinged. But, plunder his memory as Alexio did, he could not recall meeting any other woman that night. Apart from the housekeeper who had shown him to his suite while he'd still been seething with thwarted fury over her employer's offensive amusement at his guest's refusal to sleep with a whore.

'Let me refresh your memory,' Sander Christoulakis breathed in some discomfiture, evidently having hoped that his son would recall the young woman without the prompting of the photograph he now set down on the table.

Alexio focused on the photo with incredulity and instant recognition. He muttered a sudden curse and reached for it. Having been taken in profile, it was not a very good shot, but he remembered that submissive bent head, that pale hair pulled back in a severe style and those fragile facial features.

'I thought she was the housekeeper!' Alexio confessed with a sound of frank disbelief. 'She behaved like one, *not* like the daughter of the house! Gakis snapped his fingers and she appeared and he spoke to her as if she was a servant. That timid little thing was Ione Gakis?'

'Minos did say that she's quiet and shy.'

'Colourless and mousey,' Alexio countered with ruthless bite, but a faint dark line of colour now scored his sculpted cheekbones and he swung away for, even in the mood he had been in that evening, he had not been impervious to her natural appeal.

He remembered her all too well: the delicacy of her fine features, eyes as green as emeralds and as startling and unexpected in a Greek woman as her fair colouring. A beauty without artifice and the absolute antithesis of the voluptuous and artificial party girls paraded before him by his host. He had never made a pass at a servant in his life but only her silent formality and his own innate sense of fair play had haltered him.

'I understand that Ione has hardly ever been off that island. Her father believes in keeping his womenfolk at home,' Sander Christoulakis remarked with the wry fascination of a man who had a wife and two daughters, who thought nothing of flying all over Europe merely to visit friends or shop.

'At some time in the future, I may well consider a marriage of convenience,' Alexio conceded, his beautiful mouth hardening on the smouldering reflection that Ione Gakis should have immediately identified herself to him. 'But I have no interest in marrying Gakis's oddball daughter. At the very least I would like a wife with some personality.'

'A little personality can go a long way.' Unwilling to surrender what he saw as a fantastic opportunity for his son, Sander argued with greater vehemence. 'And before you criticise Ione Gakis for what she lacks, ask yourself what *you* have to offer a woman.'

'In what way?' Alexio intoned very drily.

'If you have no heart to give, only a fortune hunter will want to marry you,' the older man warned in frustration. 'Your current reputation as a womaniser is sufficient to make most of our friends extremely reluctant to let their daughters come into contact with you.'

'But then I'm not in the market for born-again virgins or ambitious social climbers. So they're very wise,' Alexio drawled with dismissive contempt.

Sander Christoulakis suppressed a heavy sigh. He had done his utmost to persuade his son to consider the benefits of such a business alliance, hoping that the challenge of becoming involved in the vast network of Gakis Holdings would tempt Alexio as nothing else might have done.

He had also believed that Alexio might be drawn by the sheer practicality of a marital arrangement that would demand so little from him on a personal basis. Spelling out the very obvious benefits of marrying a young woman who would one day inherit all that her father possessed would not have made the smallest impression.

'Minos will be insulted by a flat refusal,' Sander pointed out ruefully. 'He wants you to meet with him and discuss the proposal. What harm could that do?'

Alexio regarded his parent with the grim dark eyes that his business competitors had learned to respect but, whether he was prepared to show it or not, his interest had already been ignited by his recollection of that night on Lexos. 'I'll think it over.'

Fierce strain in her jade-green eyes, Ione checked her reflection with care in the mirror, for so formal a summons from her father was rare and intimidating.

Her pale blonde hair was scraped back from her equally pale face. Her dull dark blue dress barely hinted at the shape of the slim young body beneath and the hemline fell to below her knee. In a crowd nobody would have noticed her and that was exactly how her father believed his daughter ought to look: modest, unobtrusive, sexless. That his ideas were fifty years behind the times and out of place in a wealthy, educated family meant nothing to him for he boasted of his peasant roots and saw no reason why the outside world should intrude on his feudal island kingdom.

Indeed, Minos Gakis was a positive god in his own household. A domineering controlling man with an explosive temper that could turn to violence in the space of a moment and, to him, a woman would always be a lesser being and a possession. While she was still a very young child, Ione had learned the correct code of behaviour to observe in her father's radius and she knew well how to control her tongue and keep her head down in a storm. On more than one occasion, after all, she had seen her late mother being battered by the older man's fists, and as she'd grown up, no matter how hard Amanda Gakis had tried to protect her daughter from similar treatment, she too had suffered from his brutality.

Her bedroom door opened with jarring abruptness and without the polite warning of a prefatory knock. Flinching, Ione spun round just as her father's sister, Kalliope, appeared, her thin, sallow face sour.

'Why are you always looking at yourself in the mirror?' Kalliope snorted with derision. 'It's foolish when you're so plain. But then, had you been born a Gakis, you would have been a beauty.

Accustomed to the older woman's gibes, Ione resisted the dangerous temptation to ask what had gone wrong in Kalliope's own case, for even the kindest person would have been challenged to find attraction in those sharp features. As for that crack about her *not* having been born into the Gakis family, Ione was too well accustomed to the knowledge that she had been adopted to rise to that bait and give the older woman reason to complain to her brother that her niece had been rude to her.

Kalliope observed her brother's every household rule with religious fervour and received considerable satisfaction from reporting those unwise enough to transgress those rules. Furthermore, she liked Ione far less than she had liked Ione's mother, for, while Kalliope had continued to rule the roost over the gentle English bride her brother had taken as a wife, she had found their adopted daughter, Ione, a tougher nut to crack. Ione might not answer back and might show her aunt superficial respect. But ever since the day four years earlier, when Ione had been dragged

back kicking and screaming defiance from Athens airport,
there had been a silent stoic determination in the younger
woman's clear gaze that made Kalliope feel like an angry,
frustrated mosquito trying to sting an indifferent victim.

'Your father has exciting news for you,' Kalliope informed her curtly.

As Ione crossed the reception room beyond her bedroom in step with her aunt her pace slowed as apprehension gripped her. 'I shall look forward to hearing it.'

'Yet you've been such an ungrateful daughter,' Kalliope
told her with harsh disapproval. 'You don't deserve what
is coming to you!'

What was coming to her? Her aunt's resentment was
unconcealed and Ione's curiosity flared even higher, but
the sick knot of anxiety in her tummy only tightened. She
could never be in her father's presence without feeling fear
and he was not a man given to doling out treats. Indeed,
Ione had often wondered if her father reaped a mean pleasure from ensuring that she was invariably denied what
she most wanted. But then he did not love her, he had
never loved her, and, soon after her adoptive mother's
death, he had enjoyed telling her *why* she had been
adopted.

Amanda Gakis had given birth to a son, Cosmas, within
a year of her marriage but, in the following seven years,
she had not managed to conceive again. Desperate for a
second son, Minos Gakis had learned that sometimes after
a woman had adopted a child her unexplained infertility
could subsequently end in her becoming pregnant. In those
days, the popular view had been that, having satisfied her
longing for a baby, a woman might stop fretting and relax
and conception was then more likely to take place. Sadly,
however, Ione's arrival in the family had neglected to de-
liver the required result for her mother had not become

pregnant again. As her father had regarded his adopted daughter as no more than the means to that hopeful end, there had been little chance of her securing much of a hold on his paternal affections in that disappointing aftermath.

Her aunt left Ione standing in the echoing marble hall outside her father's office suite. Kalliope knew as well as Ione did that she would be kept waiting. Taut with strain, Ione gazed out the window, untouched by the gorgeous view of the bay that the villa overlooked. Golden sunlight and blue skies reflected on the shimmering seas of the Aegean far below. Lexos was a beautiful island and the huge, fabulous house in which she lived possessed every comfort that wealth could buy. Unfortunately, nothing could compensate Ione for the reality that she was as much a prisoner in her father's home as a criminal in an isolation cell.

The freedom she craved was as much out of her reach as it had ever been. In four endless years she had not been allowed off the island, for her father no longer trusted her. Her attempt to run away had been ill-judged and foolish, a *wasted* opportunity, she reflected with bitter hindsight, for she had not planned it well enough and had merely forewarned her father of her intentions.

At the time, she had been receiving regular orthodontic treatment in Athens, and it had been relatively easy to slip out of the dental clinic past her unsuspicious bodyguards and dive into a taxi to head to the airport. But she had not had the foresight to check the timetables in advance and had not had the wit to just buy a ticket for the first available seat on *any* international flight. No, her goal had been London and she had sat around like a fool awaiting that flight only to be cornered and forced from the airport by her bodyguards before the plane had even landed. She shuddered at the recollection of the welcome home she had received from her outraged and incredulous father, who had never dreamt until that day that she might dare to try and escape his bullying tyranny.

After all, her mother never had. But then any spirit Amanda Gakis had ever had had been crushed out of her by her husband's sneering verbal attacks and even more punishing fists.

'Where would I go?' her adoptive mother had once asked Ione with open disbelief when her teenage daughter had suggested that leaving her abusive marriage was the only solution to her unhappiness. 'How would I live? Wherever I went, your father would find me. He would never let me leave…he loves me too much!'

Love, Ione thought with a pained cynicism far beyond her years. Love had made a victim of the beautiful mother she had adored. Love had been one of Amanda's favourite excuses for the violence she had accepted as her lot in her life, along with the stress of her husband's workaholic ways on his temperament and her own inexcusable stupidity. She had blamed herself. Even while she had lain terminally ill, she had blamed herself for lingering long enough to distress and inconvenience her husband and her son.

Eyes stinging as she realised just how much she still missed the woman whose love had cocooned her from the worst of her father's abuse, Ione stiffened with dread as the older man's smooth executive assistant emerged with a surprisingly unctuous smile on his face.

'Miss Gakis…come this way.'

Minos Gakis stood below his own flattering portrait in the lofty-ceilinged room. He was a big thickset man with an imposing presence but he had yet to recover the weight he had shed while he was being treated for cancer. Indeed, although his illness had been a well-kept secret and had been successfully treated, his harsh features looked even more lined and gaunt to her than they had months earlier and his complexion was the colour of putty. For the very first time, it occurred to Ione that his recovery seemed much slower than might have been expected for a man of his former health and vigour.

'Are you well, Papa?' she heard herself ask in instinctive dismay, for it had been several weeks since she had seen him as he had been abroad on business.

'I can see that my caring, compassionate daughter will be sadly missed in this household,' Minos responded with cutting amusement.

Embarrassed colour washed over Ione's pallor and only a second later did she begin wondering where she could possibly be going that she might be missed. Hope sprang up in her in so fast and strong a surge that her knees trembled as she stood there. Had he finally forgiven her for trying to run away? Was he now willing to consider allowing her to lead a more normal life?

'After all these years, you are *finally* going to be of some use to me,' the burly older man informed her with satisfaction.

Ione stiffened, recognising the foolish aspect of her wild hopes of being permitted a life of her own. When had her father ever done anything that had pleased her? He had broken down at her mother's graveside, but her surprise and relief that he had shown that amount of humanity had been ruined by her painful memories of the mental and physical damage he had inflicted on a woman who had never hurt another living soul by word or by deed.

'I have found you a husband,' Minos announced and paused for effect.

The shock of that revelation rocked Ione on her feet and, though she struggled not to betray any reaction, a faint gasp was muffled low in her throat. Her heart was racing but her keen mind was racing even faster. A husband? Why on earth would he find her a husband? There had to be a reason. It would *have* to be of profit to him in some way. She knew better than to utter a single question or exclamation for he would react to either response as if she had been impertinent.

'Speak when you are spoken to,' had been a lesson etched into Ione's soul during childhood. 'A respectful daughter does not question a parent.'

The silence lay like concrete slowly setting her feet into greater rigidity while she waited for him to speak again. A husband, she thought with dazed incredulity. Why had she not foreseen such a possibility? Well, principally she had not anticipated the development because she was painfully aware that her father revelled in keeping his family at his beck and call and wholly dependent on him in every way.

'If Cosmas had not died,' the older man stated with harsh exactitude as he referred to her older brother, who had been killed when his private plane had crashed the year before, 'I would have scorned any thought of making such a marriage for you. But you are all that I have now and some day you will inherit Gakis Holdings.'

If his first announcement had shaken her, that second made her lips part in shock and she whispered, '*I'm*…to be your heir?'

He vented a sardonic laugh. 'Who else is left? In the eyes of the law, you are my daughter even though you do not possess a single drop of my blood.'

Yet she was proud that she was not a Gakis, relieved that she need never fear the taint of his genes, and she stood there lost in her own increasingly frantic thoughts. She did not *want* to inherit Gakis Holdings. His huge international business empire was the monster that had created his unfettered power. Enormous wealth had made him untouchable. Without hesitation, he destroyed those who antagonised him and his sphere of influence stretched terrifyingly far and wide. Time and time again the greed of others had protected him for he bribed those who might have exposed his corrupt business methods…or even what went on in his own home.

Perspiration beaded her short upper lip as she registered the peculiar direction of her thoughts at that particular moment. Her father had just told her that he had found her a husband. Why wasn't she thinking about the shattering statement? As the silence buzzed around her she felt faint and sick and the sound of her own heartbeat seemed to be thundering in her own ears.

Suddenly she understood *why* she could not dwell on the news that she was to be married off like some medieval bride without any right to have a say in her own future. What was the point of agonising over what she could not prevent? For if she defied him, he would hurt her and harm what mattered most to her. He was remorseless and the process of intimidation would begin the instant she voiced a word of objection. He had turned her into a coward, a lousy, grovelling thing without the guts to take on a fight she knew she could not win.

'I'm impressed,' Minos Gakis informed her with a quietness of tone that sent a cold shiver down her rigid spine. 'You know your place in life now. That's good, for I won't take any nonsense over this matter. As your father, I know what is best for you.'

'Yes, Papa,' she muttered sickly.

'Don't you even want to know who your husband will be?' he mocked, revelling in her submission to his dictates.

'If you want to tell me,' she intoned half under her breath.

'Alexio Christoulakis.'

Her knees almost gave beneath her in shock. She glanced up and encountered her father's cold look of amusement. 'Alexio...Christoulakis?'

Slowly, painfully slowly, her triangular face drenched with colour for she recalled the night she had met Alexio Christoulakis with too great a clarity for comfort. Her long, naturally dark lashes dropped again to conceal her transfixed gaze. Alexio Christoulakis...the *numero uno* womaniser, who seemed addicted to making headlines in both the business section and the society pages. The guy who didn't like to sleep on satin sheets and who had insisted she changed them even though it had been the early hours of the morning. The guy whose bride-to-be had drowned in a drunken moonlit swim. The guy who had treated her like a maid and barely registered that she was human. The guy who was so achingly beautiful to look at she had stared and stared in spite of herself every chance she had got...

'I'm not surprised that you can hardly credit your good fortune,' Minos Gakis murmured unpleasantly. 'But I'm sure I don't need to add that you need not look for fidelity from him. This is a business arrangement. He will take the place that your brother once occupied and as your husband he will become part of this family.'

With his every successive word the blood in her veins chilled more. He was spelling out the brutal facts. She would only be the means by which Alexio Christoulakis could be put in a position of trust as a son-in-law.

'He's brilliant, single-minded, strong. It took a lot to persuade him to agree to this alliance. But I *need* him. When he arrives tomorrow, you will do whatever it takes to keep him content. Is that understood?' her father pressed coldly.

Pinning bloodless lips together, she nodded jerkily. 'Yes, Papa.'

'Even when you become his wife, your first loyalty will remain with me. You will not tell him that you are adopted. The Christoulakis family take great pride in their family tree. You will not embarrass or offend them with the news that you were born illegitimate *or* reveal that you have a twin sister, who is nothing more than a common prostitute. Nor will you again seek contact with her. Is that also understood?'

A faint shudder rippled through Ione's slight frame until she pulled herself taut again. Bitter revulsion and anger currented through her but it was backed by despair. She saw how her future was being mapped out: a future that would be as confined and empty as the present. He expected her to marry a stranger and spy on him for his benefit. He was demanding that she go on living a lie for he did not want it to be known that macho Minos Gakis had adopted his daughter, rather than sired her himself. And to drive the knife in harder, he abused the twin she had never met, scorning her sister for her lifestyle. Hatred made her very lungs burn and she turned her head away.

'Answer me, Ione,' he growled.

'Yes, Papa. I understand,' she said with all the expression of a robot.

The instant the interview was at an end, she headed straight for the gymnasium. There she changed into an exercise outfit and embarked on a rigorous training session to empty her taut, shivering body of stress. She overdid it and exhausted herself, finally slumping down on a mat, damp and shaking, to stare at the floor. And it was only then, at the last expected moment, that she finally grasped *why* she should be greeting the announcement of her approaching nuptials with joy and relief...

The minute that she left the island with her bridegroom would simply be the countdown to her eventual escape from the whole darned lot of them! Ione flung back her pale blonde head and her laughter suddenly echoed across the big empty gym. Alexio Christoulakis would be her passport to *freedom*, not her future keeper, not yet another lord and master in her life.

Having had experience of one bullying, aggressive male, she had no intention of accepting a second. But it was essential that Alexio marry her just to get her off Lexos. Not even her father was likely to suspect that she might choose to walk out on her bridegroom *after* her wedding. Especially not when it came to a male as eligible and good-looking as Alexio Christoulakis, who was rumoured to be the top pin-up in girls' schools across the globe.

Ione began to smile, soft mouth curving as she flung herself back on the padded mat and started to plan. When she reached England she would find her sister, Misty, for although it had been more than four years since that letter had arrived from her twin she still remembered every line of the address on it. Fossetts, her sibling's foster home had been called, and surely from that point it would be a simple matter to trace Misty even if she no longer lived there. Yet her own sister knew nothing about her, not even her present name, Ione acknowledged ruefully. At birth Ione had been given the name Shannon, but Amanda Gakis had chosen a new name for her adopted daughter. However, when she did finally get to meet her long-lost twin she really would have to work out some very tactful, very, very kind way of persuading her elder sister that she did not need to be the victim of rich, using, abusing men.

*   *   *

As the helicopter came in to land over Lexos, Alexio was thinking about the disconcerting meeting he had had with Minos Gakis forty-eight hours earlier and the commitment he had made in agreeing to marry Ione.

After having advanced an extremely advantageous business partnership that had taken Alexio by surprise, Gakis had laid *all* his cards on the table. In telling Alexio the truth about his health, the older man had to a very great extent put himself in Alexio's power, for the news that the billionaire tycoon might only have a few months left to live would send shock waves crashing through the business world and cause a steep fall in the value of the shares in Gakis Holdings, making it vulnerable to a takeover bid.

The Gakis empire ran only with Minos Gakis at the helm. His senior executives had been picked not for their ability to think on their feet but for the efficiency in following orders without question. Minos did indeed need a second-in-command, a son-in-law bound by family ties to hold the fort while he went into hospital for further treatment. For if he did *not* emerge again, what would happen to a daughter raised like a convent novice on an island and without the smallest grasp of what the real world was like? A young woman who would inherit billions and become the target of every smooth-talking greedy fortune hunter across the globe?

But without a doubt, Gakis was sick in more than body, a father jealous of his precious little girl's affections, for why else should he have raised his daughter in such unnatural isolation? Almost twenty-three and never had a boyfriend? Was Minos Gakis crazy? Didn't he realise that his daughter would fall madly in love with the first man who gave her some attention?

That's likely to be *you*, Alexio's intelligence told him

and, even though women who clung and looked at him with adoration turned him off big time, the shadow of a faint smile touched the corners of his strong mouth. Ione would be his wife, after all, and she had not looked like the demanding type. Different horses for different courses, he reflected with cool confidence. If she loved him their marriage of convenience might well run a great more smoothly. But what kind of a woman allowed herself to be bartered off like a commodity?

The 'commodity' in question was engaged in equally careful thought at that moment. Ione was working out how she could best put Alexio at ease and lull him into a false sense of security. After all, she did not want him succumbing to an attack of cold feet and spoiling her plans, and she had not forgotten her father's admission that it had taken a great deal to persuade Alexio into marrying her. She would have liked to show him that she could be a lot more presentable in appearance than her current circumstances allowed. Unfortunately that option was barred for her father might well lose his temper if she appeared wearing the cosmetics and the more flattering outfits that she sometimes put on to cheer herself up in the privacy of her bedroom.

Unfortunately, the only thought in Alexio Christoulakis's head when he first looked at her would be…sex. Her nose wrinkled. He would wonder what she would be like in bed; he wouldn't be able to help himself. He was Greek, he was *very* oversexed. And he had made an outsize fool of himself two years ago over a greedy little tart of a show-off with nothing else going for her but her ability to show her boobs and bare bottom off in public on a monotonously regular basis. Face it, she would be dealing with a very basic, testosterone-driven male, who left his supposedly brilliant brain outside the bedroom door. And here she was looking as plain and sexless as it was possible to look and he might well take fright. So she had to draw him in...*somehow*, ensure he got the impression that, no matter how devoid of instant appeal she might seem, the wedding night at least was likely to be a wow.

Of course, she didn't plan on sticking around for the wedding night, but he could have no suspicion of that reality. But then, he deserved *all* that he had coming to him, didn't he? What kind of a man agreed to marry a woman as part of a cold-blooded, callous business deal? A sexist, domineering, ruthless, power-hungry, insensitive pig!

As Alexio Christoulakis emerged from the helicopter he was gilded by bright sunlight. The selfish, spoilt pig who had demanded that she change his wretched bed sheets at two o'clock in the morning, Ione reminded herself as she stood like a small, rigid statue by her burly father's side.

But she had chosen to forget the sheer raw impact of Alexio in the flesh and the closer he got, the less she breathed and her chest tightened, for he *was* so incredibly good-looking. The golden light shimmered over the luxuriant blue-black hair cropped to his arrogant head, accentuated his superb bone structure, the stunning dark, deepset eyes, the bold brows, aggressive jawline and wide, charismatic mouth. His pearl-grey business suit was cut to fit wide shoulders, lean hips and long, powerful thighs that required no helpful enhancement from his tailor. He strolled towards them not one whit put out by a reception committee and a situation that would have filled ninety-nine out of a hundred men with a sizeable degree of discomfiture.

Her own heart was hammering with nervous tension and, had she not been holding herself taut with the self-discipline of years of training, she would have trembled. His vibrant self-assurance infuriated her, but on another level she could only be impressed by that show of strength, that cool, contained tough front. One wrong move, one word out of place and her father would ruin him. Didn't he realise that he was walking into the lion's den? Didn't he appreciate that if he married into the Gakis family he would be selling his soul to the devil?

'Ione...' Alexio looked down into eyes the same shade as precious jade, the most unreadable female eyes he had ever met, utterly empty of any impression, and the smooth and polished greeting ready on his tongue somehow died there. She had the pale, still face of a madonna, possessed of pure, perfect symmetry and...untouchable. At a distance she had looked like a doll, now she bore a very close resemblance to an ice statue: frigid from head to toe. The wedding night promised to be a *real* challenge.

'Alexio...' Ione squeezed out his name in acknowledgement, straining with all her might to get enough oxygen back to manage that feat.

Alexio watched the flow of warm pink colour burnish her cheeks, the uncertain flutter of her silky brown lashes and the brief relaxation of her taut lipline into soft, sexy fullness as she spoke. As he noted the tiny pulse beating out her tension below her delicate collar-bone, he recognised that she was neither indifferent nor cold, but raw with nerves and struggling to hide the fact. A primal sense of satisfaction lancing through him, his slow, dangerous smile curved his handsome mouth...

CHAPTER TWO

'BRING us coffee…' Minos Gakis rapped out to Ione the instant the three of them entered the air-conditioned cool of the villa.

Conscious of Alexio's veiled surprise at that harsh demand, Ione reddened. It was an effort at that instant to recall what mattered most, for somehow being treated like an object of derision in Alexio's presence hit her even harder than usual. However, suppressing her embarrassment, Ione pushed her head up high and lifted her slight shoulders back. Praying that her father was too busy talking to notice, she walked down the long marble hall with small, slow, measured steps that made her slim hips sway in what she hoped was a subtle but enticing manner.

She knew how experienced women practised such small visual wiles on the male sex. Goodness knew, she had had ample opportunity to observe the behaviour of the voluptuous giggling blondes her father brought over to Lexos when he entertained. Of course, on such occasions she was supposed to behave as though she were quite unaware of what went on in her own home and keep to her own wing of the villa, but as the years had passed Minos Gakis had become less discreet. She had often seen those women basking round the pool and had watched them switch on the seductive charm to attract lustful male visitors. Her soft mouth tightened with helpless distaste.

Engaged in listening to his host, Alexio watched Ione progress down the hall, a faint hint of a frownline marking his winged black brows as he questioned his own reluctance to take his attention from her. The fluid slowness of her walk attracted his gaze first to the intrinsically feminine curve of her *derrière* and then to the soft rise of her hemline above her slender, shapely legs. She moved with the grace of a dancer but it was another, far more disturbing quality that caused the sudden startling ache of fullness in Alexio's groin.

Seconds later, Ione moved out of view and slumped back against the cold corridor wall, all of a quiver from the stress of a masquerade she found demeaning. But she *had* to try to engage Alexio's interest and convince him that she was content to marry him, for if he suspected otherwise he might change his mind and, if he did so, even her father couldn't force him to marry her and all hope of her getting off the island would be lost. She shivered at that awareness. Yet to attempt for the first time ever to attract a man and to do so in her father's vicinity demanded a degree of courageous subtlety she feared she did not possess.

She had worked so hard at forgetting just how unnerving a personality Alexio Christoulakis was, Ione acknowledged uneasily as she collected the already prepared coffee tray. His arrival had shaken her up a lot more than she had expected. With reluctance, she recalled their first brief encounter.

That night a couple of months earlier she had been relieved to be mistaken for an employee, for it was humiliating to be treated like a servant by her father in front of his discomfited guests. Alexio had been in too much of a rage to be more discerning, she recalled abstractedly. Dark eyes blazing gold with fierce pride, aggressive jawline hard as iron. And she had had a very fair idea of what hoops her father had put him through for his own amusement.

But she had still been struck as dumb as a tongue-tied schoolgirl when she'd first laid eyes on Alexio Christoulakis. Even though she had seen those same lean, dark, handsome features in the magazines she read, he had always looked so impossibly cool and reserved. She had not been prepared for a male so vibrant and so volatile in the flesh that raw energy literally sizzled from him.

And when he had called her back to change those satin sheets that her aunt believed to be the last word in sophistication, she had had no need to make that her own personal task for the villa had staff on duty twenty-four hours a day. Yet inexplicably she had hurried off to fetch fresh linen. When she had returned to his bedroom, he had been standing by the open doors onto the balcony, exuding a ferocious tension that had sent her own sensory processes into overload.

Guilty as a sneak thief but unable to resist her own fascination, she had kept on stealing covert glances at him. It had taken her for ever to make up the bed again, for her hands had been all fingers and thumbs. But he had seemed indifferent to her lingering presence and her lack of dexterity. Only once had their eyes met head-on and her mouth had run dry as she'd fallen victim to those spectacular golden eyes. A split second later he had swung away as though he were alone and had strode out onto the balcony where he had remained until she had departed again.

As she emerged from that unsettling recollection, perspiration beaded Ione's short upper lip. As she entered the main salon with the laden tray, she could see the shaded, vine-encrusted loggia outside where her father was seated in regal splendour and her heart sank at his choice of location. Evidently impervious to any fear of heights, Alexio was lounging back against the low retaining wall that was built into the very edge of the cliff, the relaxed angle of his lean, powerful frame pronounced.

Ione's hands clenched bone-white round the tray handles as she attempted to blank out the panoramic view and forestall the sick sense of dizzy terror that always threatened her in the loggia.

His keen gaze narrowing with questioning force on her drawn face, Alexio straightened and strode forward. 'Let me take that for you.'

Dismayed that he had broken off the conversation to offer her assistance, Ione froze. She collided with gleaming dark golden eyes fringed with dense black lashes and her heart seemed to crash inside her. He detached her death grip from the tray and strolled back to set it on the stone table. Screening her bemused gaze, she edged as close to the house wall as she dared to reach the table and serve the coffee.

'You're afraid of heights,' Alexio murmured.

Minos Gakis said drily, 'She must overcome it.'

Conscious of her father's annoyance that she should have interrupted their dialogue, Ione breathed jerkily, 'It's foolish, irrational. I mustn't give way to it.'

Alexio studied her. She was making a valiant effort to control her fear but she was as white as a sheet and the coffee-pot was shaking in her hand. And her father? He was smiling. Alexio had a sudden primal desire to tip his host out of his seat and suspend him upside down over that fearsome drop to kill that smile. It was an urge that shook him.

Ione sank down into the closest chair and struggled to get a grip on herself again. Accustomed as she was to being ignored in her father's company, she focused on Alexio while the two men talked business, and she reflected on what a poor impression she must have made in betraying her terror of heights. Hardly the right way to connect with a male once fabled for his taste in dangerous sports. He had the most amazing eyelashes, she thought, losing her concentration to momentarily dwell on the lush black sweep visible in his hard, angular profile.

As Alexio sent her a winging glance, brilliant dark golden eyes flaring into connection with hers, a surge of inflaming heat tremored through Ione in a shock wave of response. Her teeth set together as her breath caught in her throat and she tore her attention from him again. Highspots of colour formed over her cheekbones as she fought her own instinctive reaction to his raw masculinity with shamed and angry resentment.

She had no intention of following in her unfortunate mother's footsteps and letting her body rule over her brain. So he was gorgeous, but what was that worth? She had recognised her own foolish susceptibility three months earlier and had despised herself for her weakness. A womanising louse like Alexio Christoulakis figured nowhere in the future she craved. No man was going to break her heart. No man was going to control her. Once she had her freedom, if anybody broke hearts, it was going to be her. That ambition in mind, Ione curled back into her chair, arched her back a little and shifted her slim legs to let her hemline ride up ever so slightly.

Conscious of her every move, Alexio was entertained by her attempt to portray herself as a sensually exciting woman by exposing an inch of flesh above her knee, and he was equally conscious that her every provocative move was studied. Was she trying to turn him off the idea of marrying her? Or turn him onto it? Whichever, he was already appreciating that that smooth madonna face was deceptive.

Angling her blonde head back, Ione lowered her lashes

and let the tip of her tongue slide out to dampen her lower lip. His gaze zeroed in on her, black lashes screening his shimmering eyes to linger on the darting pink tip moistening her full, inviting mouth. Amusement ebbing, his lean, hard body clenched on a surge of sexual hunger strong enough to infuriate him. Why was she playing games with him?

Minos Gakis rose upright, his heavy movements betraying his weariness. 'I must attend to business, Alexio... Ione will entertain you. We'll discuss the wedding arrangements over dinner.

Ione was startled by that speech. If wedding arrangements were to be discussed, then their marriage was *already* a foregone conclusion. As it seemed that Alexio must have agreed to marry her even before he'd arrived on Lexos, her attempts to make herself seem more attractive had been a ludicrous waste of time and energy. On Alexio's terms, her true worth lay in her Gakis surname and her future dowry, not in her looks or her individuality. Her cheeks blossomed with chagrined colour. Once again she had been made to feel the sting of her own essential unimportance, but she realised that it would be unwise to suddenly abandon the act she had been putting on for his benefit.

'Shall we go inside?' Alexio drawled, taking charge with all-male decisiveness.

But for the reality that sitting out in the loggia was a punishment to her, Ione might have disagreed. Looking up at him to note how very, very tall he was from that angle, and filled with almost childish resentment by the intimidating nature of that fact, she got up with a nod.

Sudden angry suspicion gripped Alexio as he stood back to let Ione precede him indoors, his glinting appraisal resting on her undeniably sensual gliding walk across the terracotta tiles. How did he know that Ione Gakis wasn't a raving nymphomaniac with a father desperate to marry her off before she engulfed the family in scandal? If that were the case, the Gakis billions would be equal to preventing the spread of damaging rumours, but not the most optimistic of men could hope to hide such a shame for ever. The constant references to Ione's shyness and her protected upbringing added to her dowdy appearance might just be ploys to convince him that she was what her father said she was. But how could he know for sure? How did he *know* he wasn't being suckered into marriage with a woman who might try to make the Christoulakis name a laughing stock?

'Your father was a little premature in his reference to wedding arrangements,' Alexio imparted, smooth as velvet. 'I did tell him that you and I would have to talk before anything could be finalised.'

Ione stiffened, her nervous tension reawakening in a dismayed surge as she registered that she still had to win him over. Flustered, she muttered unwarily, 'I should've guessed. Papa…Papa can be impatient. He makes assumptions.'

'Which of us doesn't?' Alexio rested a light hand to her spine to guide her out of the bright sunlight into the vast salon and she was so ridiculously aware of his touch, his very proximity, that she imagined she felt his fingers burn through the dress fabric into the taut skin of her back. 'But you intrigue me. I'm not sure what to make of you.'

Something akin to panic shrilled through Ione. What was that supposed to mean? Intrigue? Didn't that suggest something covert? Did he suspect that her efforts to attract him were just one big empty pretence? How could he not? How could she possibly have believed that she could fool a guy who had slept with dozens of women into crediting that she would ever be a wow in bed?

'You don't know me,' Ione pointed out tightly, an unsteady hand sliding down over her dress to smooth it as she braced herself to try and redress the damage by reassuring him. 'But I can be *anything* you want me to be.'

The fall of silence that greeted that impulsive announcement was instant and it worked on her nerves like a chainsaw.

Taken aback by that startling assurance, Alexio frowned, dark golden eyes narrowing below winged ebony brows as he stared at her.

'I just don't know what you want from me yet,' Ione stated, gathering steam from the sheer level of fear holding her rigid, for if she had blown any hope of him wanting to marry her with her silly play-acting, she had *nothing* left to lose. Not only would her father lose his head with her, but she would also be buried alive on Lexos for years to come.

'What I want from you?' Alexio prompted in fascination, having recognised the spark of panic in her wide green eyes before she'd veiled them and the extent of the tension keeping her so still.

'I need to know what you want,' Ione told him again. 'Maybe you don't want me interfering in your life if we get married. That's fine. I *won't*. You don't need to worry about that. I'm a very practical person. Very quiet too. You'll hardly know I'm there. Once I know what you like, everything will be as you expect it to be.'

A shaken surge of angry compassion stirred in Alexio. Anger at her father for giving her the impression that such assurances would be necessary and compassion that she should feel driven to humble herself in such a way for his benefit. 'I have only one question that needs an answer. Do *you* want to be my wife?'

Eyes lowering, Ione trembled, compressed her lips, parted them again. An obvious question, one she should have foreseen but harder to answer than she could ever have dreamt, for by nature she was not a liar. And when she lifted her lashes and collided with the dark golden intensity of his questioning gaze, her breath feathered in her throat and her breasts seemed to swell inside her cotton bra. Embarrassment scythed through her as her nipples tightened into straining buds and an arrow of heat speared low in her pelvis. Yet *still* she could not take her eyes from his lean, dark, devastating features.

'Ione…I'm aware that your father has a forceful personality. If you feel in any way pressured into this—'

'Oh, no!' Ione broke in hurriedly, keen to make that denial for she could now see the direction in which the dialogue was going. 'How could you think that?'

'I don't know what to think,' Alexio said with the frankness that as a rule he only employed within his own family circle, his brilliant gaze pinned to her with penetrating force. 'I'm getting mixed signals from you.'

Sentenced to stillness by the sheer mesmeric effect of those beautiful eyes, Ione murmured half under her breath and without really knowing where the words had come from. 'I want to marry you more than anything else in the world.'

Darker colour accentuated Alexio's fabulous cheekbones for he had not expected that emotive a declaration. 'Why?' he heard himself say as if what she had just said was still not enough, though it was.

'I had a picture of you in my locker at boarding-school.' Her fair skin drenched with pink as she forced out that statement. 'Everybody had a pin-up. You were mine.'

Initially disconcerted at the news that he had been the focus of a schoolgirl crush, Alexio suddenly found himself smiling, and it was a smile full of so much natural charisma that it turned Ione's knees to cotton wool beneath her.

Gotcha, Ione thought with intense satisfaction in spite of that smile. He had fallen for it. And why not? The target of admiring and awestruck women all his adult life, he was accustomed to flattery. Actually, it had been one of her classmates who had languished over him at fifteen. Ione had thought love from afar was childish and a waste of energy and had kept cute photos of her dog inside her locker.

'I suppose we have to start somewhere,' Alexio conceded with a husky laugh of amusement.

Losing every suspicion of her motives, he castigated himself for the wildness of his own suspicions about her morals in the loggia. Her honesty was refreshing but naive. But then, after the sheltered life she had led, her naivety was understandable. In times to come, though, she might look back and hate him for having listened to that gauche little declaration, for what did he have to offer her in return? In the material line, nothing, and he didn't like that. Indeed, he had already decided how best to deal with that potential problem.

'I believe that our marriage will work best if you settle your future inheritance on any children we might have and we live on my income,' Alexio spelt out without hesitation.

Suddenly, Ione was grateful she had no plans to become a kept woman. He was *so* Greek: he wanted a dependant wife. How dared he suggest that she consent to that kind of an agreement merely to conserve his precious male pride? In her place, what man would agree to such an arrangement? It did not seem to occur to him that she might already be wealthy in her own right, yet Ione had inherited considerable funds from both her mother and her brother. As for having children with him, since the possibility was not going to arise, she didn't even think about it.

'Ione...I appreciate that that will be a very difficult decision for you to make, but I would like you to give serious consideration to the idea,' Alexio continued with level cool.

'I'll think about it,' Ione responded with castdown eyes. Love in a cottage Christoulakis-style? Had she been born of Gakis blood and truly intending to be his wife, at that point, all negotiations would have broken down. But money had no power over her, for immense wealth had brought her adoptive family nothing but misery.

His strong jawline clenched, dark golden eyes challenging. 'Your father will disapprove but I won't allow him to interfere in our marriage. You must accept that too.'

'Yes, of course.' But at that aggressive announcement of intent, Ione almost released a shuddering sigh of relief over the escape she was planning on. What Alexio had just said was grounds for a battle royal. Minos Gakis was no fond parent, but he set great store on his own pride and he would be outraged if his daughter was seen to live in anything less than a palace. But then the situation would never develop, she reminded herself impatiently, for her relationship with Alexio would not last beyond their wedding day. Furthermore, Alexio was only dictating terms for what was essentially a business deal rather than a marriage.

'I need you to voice your own opinions.' Exasperation currented through Alexio as she stood there like a slender statue revealing nothing of her thoughts.

No, he didn't. Since when had impervious demands required opinions? Ione regarded him from below curling brown lashes, green eyes cloaked, for every time she looked at him she was struck anew by his lethal dark attraction. 'But I agree with everything you've said.'

'You *must* have requests to make of me,' Alexio informed her.

'I would love to spend our honeymoon in Paris,' Ione dared, her low-pitched voice a tad uneven for so much was riding on his response. 'I believe you have a house there.'

'I also have a very beautiful villa in the Caribbean.'

Even that one little thing, he had to argue about, Ione thought fiercely. He couldn't help himself. An inability to give way gracefully to any will other than their own was the essential flaw in all ruthless, successful men. Well, whether he liked it or not, he was going to Paris. He *had* to take her to a city so that she could leave him. Staging a nifty vanishing act from a potentially remote Caribbean villa might well prove to be too great a challenge for her.

In some surprise, Alexio picked up on the antagonistic sparks in her silence. 'We could go sailing.'

'I get seasick,' Ione lied in a wooden little voice that concealed her panic at what was an even worse suggestion.

Paris. Paris where he had spent so much time with Crystal, Alexio reflected in instinctive recoil, but then he looked at Ione and, seeing the anxious light in her upward glance, he felt like a selfish bastard for denying her what appeared to be her heart's desire. 'Paris it is, then…'

Her smile, the smile she had not let him see until that moment, lit up her whole face to a startling degree. While he gazed into her shining green eyes and experienced a tightening sensation in his groin that was becoming all too familiar in her vicinity, he decided that it would be healthier to make new memories of one of his favourite cities.

'Let me show you round the picture gallery,' Ione suggested, daring to take the lead now that her battle was won and her worst fears vanquished.

Instead and without warning, Alexio reached for her and drew her close, his lean hands linking with hers and then releasing them to glide with smooth expertise up to her slim shoulders. 'First…'

No, no, no, *no*! Screamed through Ione's brain. Touching was absolutely not allowed. She stiffened, froze from head to toe, putting out defensive signals that a blind man could have sensed.

'You don't need to be nervous,' Alexio soothed in his dark velvet drawl, that roughened timbre setting up a chain-reaction echo down her rigid spine. But he knew he was lying. Every time she froze around him, he wanted to smash down her barriers, storm an attack through her defences and watch those beautiful eyes drown in him, cling to him, *hunger* for him.

She collided with smouldering golden eyes that made her head spin and her heart skip a beat in shock. She meant to step back out of reach but instead she found herself concentrating on just catching her breath. It shook her even more to feel her body wanting to push forward into the hard, all-male muscularity of his, for the rigorous control that had always been her saviour was nowhere to be found.

'Alexio…' Her own voice sounded strange to her, almost placatory.

He brought his wide, sensual mouth drifting down onto hers and then, with rueful amusement sounding deep in his throat, he pried her sealed lips apart with the tip of his tongue and explored the moist interior of her tender mouth. As the explosion of sensual sensation hit her she shuddered in its grip, her slim body alternately tensing and dissolving in the storm of physical feelings firing through her skincells. Crushed against the unyielding wall of his chest, her breasts pinched tight into throbbing peaks and the ache that stirred at the very heart of her almost hurt.

Alexio lifted his arrogant dark head to gaze down into her dreamy, bemused eyes with a sense of achievement entirely new to him. 'Am I the first?'

Having yet to regain mastery over herself in that moment and stunned by her own galloping heartbeat and excitement, Ione mumbled. 'The first to kiss me? No...'

In an abrupt movement, Alexio freed her. Who was she trying to kid? She hadn't even known *how* to kiss until he had shown her! But the dreaminess in her eyes had dissipated and she had lost colour. Indeed, she spun away from him as if he no longer existed for her and, registering that withdrawal, he immediately suspected the most likely cause.

'Who was he?' Alexio demanded, seized by a sudden dark anger that inflamed him into an instantaneous reaction.

Pale as death in the aftermath of that unwise admission, Ione could have bitten her own tongue out. Wounding memories were attacking her from all sides, but fear had risen uppermost again. If her father found out that she had mentioned Yannis, he would be furious. She did not consider Alexio's anger abnormal. Her father was a hypocrite too, preaching female purity one moment and taking solace with tarts the next.

'He was a fisherman's son. It was over two years ago. He k-kissed me. That's all,' she lied shakily.

Alexio's lean, powerful hands closed back into fists and slowly uncoiled again. Why shouldn't she have kissed

someone else? And it was such a pathetic little confession
that he was momentarily ashamed of himself for forcing
it out of her. He could not explain the strength of his own
irrational anger, and then he looked at her afresh and noted
that she had turned a sort of sickly shade, her eyes refusing
to meet his. That seething anger came out of nowhere at
him again. He recognised that he wasn't hearing the whole
story and was torn by a primitive desire to drag all the
rest of it out of her as well, for her pallor told him that
that fisherman's son had been a major event in her life.

CHAPTER THREE

'LET'S go and see those pictures,' Alexio breathed in a raw undertone. So he was unaccustomed to the experience of a woman reeling out of his arms to think about another man. But, in the circumstances, he knew his anger was unreasonable.

Ione was trembling. 'Please don't mention what I said to my father.'

Alexio flung her an astonished glance from his brilliant eyes and his jawline hardened. 'Of course not.'

Ione led the way to the ultra-modern picture gallery but her tummy was still churning. Yannis had been her first and only love and it had been sweet and innocent and harmless until the day that she'd been followed and her father's henchmen had forced her to watch as Yannis had been beaten to a pulp. Soon afterwards his family had left the island. She would never forget what *her* foolishness had cost *him*.

And what even greater foolishness it had been to admit to her bridegroom that she was not quite untouched by human hand! He was now thinking that she might not be a virgin. As she watched him view the magnificent paintings, which she believed ought to hang in a museum where at least they would be appreciated as something other than an investment, she recognised the lingering tautness in his strong, bronzed profile. Like her father, he was the contemporary equivalent of a caveman, who wanted a bride no other man had ever dared to touch. And wouldn't he just love it if she questioned him about his all-too-

40

numerous affairs? Even so, she was puzzled that he had once intended to marry a woman like Crystal Denby, whose reputation had been far from spotless.

But then Crystal had been totally, fantastically gorgeous, Ione conceded with wry acceptance. A woman blessed with such undeniable attributes got away with a great deal more than a plainer one. It must feel really good, she thought with rueful longing, to have that kind of power over a man.

'I'm sorry about the way I questioned you downstairs,' Alexio remarked in a driven undertone, swinging round without warning to level dark-as-night eyes on her triangular face. 'I have no right to question your past.'

His apology surprised her but she immediately sensed that he wanted to know more about Yannis, was indeed expecting and inviting her to respond with further details. Angry defiance stirred in her and only with the greatest difficulty did she resist the temptation to ask if he wanted to tell her about *his* lost love. Instead she simply nodded agreement in silence.

Even though she had thwarted him, grudging admiration assailed Alexio. His wide, sensual mouth slashed into a wolfish smile of acknowledgement that exuded such innate masculine power over her that she found herself smiling dizzily back at him without even thinking about it.

'I brought you this…' He drew a ring from the pocket of his beautifully tailored jacket. 'It's the Christoulakis betrothal ring, but if you don't like it it's not a problem. You can choose your own ring if you prefer to do so. I will admit upfront that my own mother considered it too old-fashioned for her taste.'

Attacked by sudden discomfiture, Ione studied the diamonds that glittered below the gallery lights. A family betrothal ring, an heirloom. A stab of guilt pierced her for, whatever she might think of his motives, he *was* on the level about their marriage and she was not. 'It's beautiful...' she muttered and she made herself extend her hand in acceptance lest she betray herself.

Alexio reached for her hand and threaded the ring onto her wedding finger. 'I may not love you but I will do everything in my power to be a good husband,' he asserted.

In receipt of that little speech, Ione gritted her teeth together. Well, it was just as well that she had no intention of hanging around to test him out on that unlikely promise! Like any other woman, she deserved to be loved and she intended to be loved by someone one day. In the meantime, she would be playing the field with loads of different boyfriends. Well, if she could get one to start with, she conceded, climbing down from her mental soapbox to allow that until she had tested herself out on the dating scene she had no idea how much man appeal she might possess.

Although a boyfriend who kissed as Alexio did would be a very good start, she acknowledged. Without a doubt, his sexual expertise had roused her own much too enthusiastic response. However, seeking to deny him that small intimacy would have been a major mistake on all fronts. And it *had* only been her hormones that had got carried away, she told herself in consolation. Since she had been deprived of almost all the natural learning experiences that she should have had with men, she might even qualify as being sex-starved. So, why should she be ashamed of the wild excitement she had felt beneath that hard, hungry mouth of his? There had really been nothing at all personal in her response to him.

'Ione...' Alexio began, studying the smooth perfection of her shuttered face and yet far-away gaze and endeavouring to fathom what had stolen her attention from him yet again.

'Alexio…how *are* you? Ione should have brought you to me immediately,' a coy female voice shrilled from the entrance to the gallery.

Sprung from her introspection by the sight of Kalliope heading for Alexio with a delighted smile on her thin face, Ione breathed in deep. She need have no further concern as to how to occupy Alexio, for her aunt, who adored young, handsome men, was more than equal to the task. And over the following hour, while he endured Kalliope's voluble enquiries about every single member of his family near and far, Alexio demonstrated the most perfect manners, patience and courtesy.

'You don't deserve a husband from a good family.' Kalliope shot her niece a look of angry resentment as the two women walked back to their own wing of the villa to change for dinner. 'If Alexio Christoulakis knew the truth about your background, *nothing* would persuade him to marry a girl from the gutter!'

For once, in receipt of her aunt's venom, Ione felt only a weary compassion. Her mother had once told her that, twenty years earlier, Kalliope had fallen in love with one of her brother's executives, but Minos Gakis had reacted in fury and had refused his permission for them to marry. Kalliope had dutifully accepted his decision and now she was in her fifties, still unmarried and bitter over the lot life had dealt her.

But at least her aunt still *had* her life, Ione reasoned with a superstitious shiver as she selected another dull dark dress from her wardrobe. Cosmas had not been so fortunate. The night that her brother had crashed his plane, he had been under enormous stress and his resulting lack of concentration had killed him. If anything, Cosmas had been even more afraid of their father than she was.

Cosmas had had the Gakis head for business laced with their mother's sensitivity. Her eyes stinging as she thought about the big brother she still missed a great deal, Ione promised herself that, no matter what it took and regardless of what deception might be involved, she would do what Cosmas had been too scared to do: she would break free, she would escape before her self-will was crushed as his had been.

The first course of the lavish dinner had been served when Minos Gakis announced that the wedding would have to take place within two weeks as business commitments would keep him out of the country during the following month. Ione's startled gaze shot to Alexio, who seemed to be absorbing the news with a lot less surprise than she was. His lean, strong face was not even tense. Indeed, he shot her a long, lingering glance from heavily lidded dark golden eyes that burned hot colour into her cheeks and made her hurriedly look away.

'The ceremony will, of course, take place here on the island,' Minos decreed and he turned to study Alexio with a half-smile. 'I see no reason why you and Ione should not then take up residence here.'

Shock powered through Ione and her fork fell from her nerveless fingers with a clatter.

'In her own home, my daughter would have the company of her aunt while you are abroad and she would also enjoy the continued security of a full protection team.'

'No...no!' Ione gasped in horror, driven into defiance by the stricken conviction that such an arrangement could only have been planned from the outset.

Even as her dismayed aunt dug warning nails into her thigh below the table, Ione's red-faced father was flying out of his chair like a jet-propelled steamroller and raising a punishing fist as he roared down at his daughter in a rage, '*What* did you say to me?'

Mutely awaiting the blow about to descend and white as milk, Ione jerked as the crash of a chair falling backward sounded from the other side of the table.

'If you lay one finger on her, I swear I'll kill you!' Alexio thundered with a raw aggression more than equal to his host's.

A silence beyond any silence that had ever fallen in the Gakis household fell at that point. Nobody had ever challenged Minos Gakis like that. Sheer disbelief had paralysed the older man's heavy features as he slowly turned his big greying head to focus on his challenger. Ione wanted to throw herself across the table and stuff the tablecloth in Alexio's big, stupid macho mouth before he got himself beaten up. What madness had come over him? Where were his much-vaunted brains when he most needed them? Her father had said that he needed Alexio but her father would *still* throw him off the island and destroy him sooner than swallow such an insult.

Minos surveyed the younger man with outraged dark eyes and hissed. 'So you think she's *your* property now…eh?'

'*Yes.*' His lean, powerful face rigid, the surge of pure black rage that had powered Alexio was still in the ascendant.

With an abruptness that made his female relatives flinch, Minos Gakis threw back his head and laughed with a derisive appreciation that curdled Ione's quivering tummy. She would call the police. No matter what it cost her, if he let his henchmen hurt Alexio, she knew that *this* time she would call the police and inform on her own father.

But a split second later, she could only watch with a

dropped jaw as her father dealt Alexio a considering look of ironic approval. 'You're a man not unlike me. Possessive, protective of what's yours. Well, then, *you* keep your mouth shut from now on!'

Ione just closed her eyes, still sick from the threat of the violence that had so nearly exploded upon them all and equally sick with humiliation. The men resumed their seats. Alexio skimmed a probing glance at Ione and asked himself if he had been guilty of a crazy overreaction, for she did not seem grateful for his intervention. He had believed that her father had been about to hit her, but it was more probable that the older man had only been waving an angry fist in the air. After all, Ione had just sat there and would surely not have done so had she feared a blow. What grounds did he have to suspect Minos of abusive behaviour? And much might be forgiven of a man fighting terminal illness and looking death in the face, Alexio reminded himself with all the discomfiture of a young and healthy male.

'I feel unwell. Please excuse me,' Ione muttered chokily.

'Yes, go,' her father growled in a tone of disgust. 'You have already done your utmost to spoil our meal!'

Ione rose on knees that felt like jelly and left the room. Her head was pounding fit to burst and all courage was failing her. Alexio would agree to them living at the villa after their wedding. Why shouldn't he? Such an arrangement would be very convenient for him. After all, it would give him complete freedom and he wouldn't need to feel guilty about leaving her for long periods with her own family. Would there even *be* a honeymoon trip now? Alexio hadn't wanted to go to Paris in the first place and her father would soon persuade him that a honeymoon was a waste of business time and energy. Tears running down her convulsed face, Ione stumbled into her bathroom and stared at herself in the vanity mirror.

What an idiot she had been to believe that she could escape her father's control of every aspect of her life! He had been way ahead of her in the planning stakes and she had been stupid not to foresee that likelihood.

Ever since that letter from her twin sister had arrived within months of her eighteenth birthday, Ione's mail had been vetted and scrutinised. Her sibling, Misty, had wanted contact with her and Ione's father had been furious that the social services had unsealed the adoption records to aid such an approach to his adopted daughter without his consent. Ione had not been allowed to answer that letter and she only knew that her sister was or had been a Sicilian tycoon's mistress because that had evidently featured in a more recent newspaper story that had come to her father's notice. She had not seen that article herself. Her father had simply informed her that the sister she longed to be reunited with was a whore.

And ever since, Ione, far from recoiling in the disgust her father had hoped to evoke in her, had been just desperate to find her twin and help her. It had been no easy task for Ione to visualise a different life from that which she had always lived, but Misty had become her focus, her sole objective. Now she could see that goal receding further and further from her and she had no idea where to turn. Weary after the long stressful day and the effects of her own overtaxed emotions, Ione showered and slid into bed.

But her sleep was restless and peppered with confused dreams. Shards of old memories mingled with the disturbing events of the day and she tossed and turned.

*   *   *

As soon as his host retired, Alexio set off immediately to find Ione.

No longer did he marvel at his bride-to-be's startling offer to be whatever *he* wanted her to be. Over twenty years in the radius of her bullying father would wear down the strongest spirit, he conceded. Understandably the very idea of having to embark on their marriage on Lexos had filled her with horror. It was natural that Ione should want her own home, even more natural that she should want to see one of the most romantic cities in the world and enjoy the freedom that had until now been denied to her. But Ione *did* need to learn one fact. His expressive mouth quirked. He was not one of her father's employees, nor was he intimidated by him.

Ought he to warn her that Minos was still a very sick man and that, far from being on the road to recovery, there was only a small chance that further surgery would extend his life? Minos wanted neither his sister nor his daughter to know the truth. What right did he himself have to interfere? Yet how could he remain silent?

A maid led him to the door of Ione's suite. He rapped on the door, waited a moment and then strode into the spacious sitting room. For a bemused moment, he thought he had walked into a toyshop for there were soft toys everywhere he looked. On shelves, on seats, grouped round tables. Teddy bears. Giant bears, medium-sized bears and small bears, some fluffy and hairy but most of them pitiful specimens, whose garments could not conceal the awful truth that they were as ancient and as bald as coots. Pinned to the spot for an instant by the onslaught of all those watching beady eyes, Alexio suppressed a groan. He was hoping the bears didn't want to travel too.

The bedroom door was open and the lamps were lit, but it was a low-pitched gasp that recaptured his attention. He strode over to the threshold. Even though it was barely eleven, Ione was in bed fast asleep. Bloody typical, was his first thought, for when did a woman ever do what you expected her to do? He had assumed that he would find her distraught and in floods of tears, but she had simply gone to bed as though the sight of her father and her bridegroom almost coming to blows over her hadn't caused her an ounce of concern!

As she shifted position a shining loop of silk pale blonde hair uncoiled and fanned across the pillows and Alexio's ruminations found a more intimate focus. She had really beautiful hair and it was much longer than he had realised. And, although her appalling dress sense by day appeared to have stopped dead somewhere around thirty years before she had even been born, by night she wore the barest minimum of peach silk that clung to every lissom curve. His attention lingering on the pouting swell of her small breasts as she arched her back in turning over, he decided he could live with maybe *one* bear.

Only as her sleep-flushed face turned towards him did he see the tracks of tears marking her fair skin, the tension still etched in her fine features. She shifted her head back and forth on the pillow while her fingers plucked at the linen sheet beneath her restive hand and her soft lips parted on a long, sighing moan of fear.

In her dream, Ione was back at the beach, her arms gripped in an imprisoning hold so that she was forced to watch every blow that Yannis withstood. She was trapped and so was he, but the responsibility was *hers* alone. Only her father could have ordered such a brutal punishment. Only her father could have instructed that his henchmen make her witness the devastation that her rebellion had unleashed.

Powerless to intervene, willing Yannis to stay down instead of stumbling upright again to invite another sickening punch from the two men set on inflicting the maximum possible damage on their victim, she flung her head and she started to scream. Over and over again, she screamed knowing that someone from the village would eventually come running, knowing that it was her only hope of bringing the brutal beating to an end.

As she came bolt upright in the bed on the back of that shrill scream her eyes flew wide and settled full of fear on the very tall, dark male shadowing her bed.

Alexio unfroze and came down on the edge of the bed in one forceful, fluid movement to close a strong arm around her. 'It was only a nightmare.'

Tremors of distress still trammelling through her slight frame, Ione jerked back from him and gasped in stricken disagreement, 'It *happened...* Yannis was beaten to a pulp!'

Unused to rejection, Alexio had stiffened, and at the mention of another man's name his lean, strong face set in formidable lines. 'What happened?' he prompted nonetheless, the need to know overruling all else.

But Ione had surfaced from her sleep-induced bewilderment and even as she bit back a sob she was wondering what Alexio was doing in her bedroom and endeavouring to pull herself together. It had been a long time since she had dreamt of that afternoon. Ione had learned in childhood to put distressing events behind her. What she could not influence, she had to tolerate.

As she flung herself back down on the tumbled pillows and flipped onto her side pale golden hair shiny as a child's obscured her drawn profile.

'What happened?' Alexio repeated as a shuddering sob tensed her again and he curved a soothing hand to her slender spine.

'I met up with Yannis secretly and Papa had him beaten up while I watched,' she whispered shakily. 'They laughed while they did it.'

Taken aback, Alexio snatched in a stark breath.

Ione shifted her head so that the glossy blonde hair tumbled back from her flushed triangular face, and unexpectedly stormy green eyes collided with his. 'He loved me and they nearly killed him for it.'

Alexio did not like what he was hearing, but other more primal responses were dulling the edge of that awareness. She was a study of unalloyed sensuality with her bright eyes and her full pink mouth and rumpled hair. Shoestring straps dissected her slim white shoulders and a fine wisp of silk defined her narrow ribcage and the provocative swell of her breasts. He hardened in urgent male response, sexual hunger flaming through him like an almost painful shot of adrenalin.

'Aren't you going to tell me that all Greek fathers have a duty to protect their daughter's virtue?' Ione pressed.

'No and not in such a way. But what future could a Gakis have with a fisherman's son?' Alexio enquired with lethal cool.

'Yannis was in his last year of med school and I had known him all my life,' Ione told him defensively.

While Alexio's intelligence warned him that the bad news about the fisherman's son was building to intolerable heights, he was simultaneously battling with a powerful urge to haul her into his arms caveman-style and imprint himself so powerfully on her that there would not be a thought in her head that did not centre solely on him.

The silence lay thick and heavy.

Ione meshed with molten-gold eyes enhanced by inky black lashes and the sudden burn of his gaze tautened her every sinew. Mouth running dry, she felt her heart thump like a trapped bird inside her as her body betrayed her. Her breasts were heavy with swollen and sensitive peaks. Heat pulsed through her in a heady tide and settled with a disturbing burn of awareness between her tensed thighs.

He bent over her, lifted a lean hand and let long brown fingers slide through her tumbled hair and curve to her cheek. Heart thundering and out of breath, she stared up at him, scanning his darkly handsome features: the proud jut of his nose, the slumbrous light in his gaze, the dark shadow of roughness accentuating his aggressive jawline and the lure of that wide, sexy mouth. Deep down in secret places she could feel herself melting like ice cream on a hot pavement and the pulse of excitement growing ever more powerful.

'You haven't even asked me what I'm doing in here,' Alexio chided huskily. 'I came to talk to you. I didn't expect you to be in bed at this hour.'

Ione swept up her hand and let her fingertips glance in an uncertain foray over the luxuriant black hair above his brow. Her own hunger electrified and terrified her, but she wanted to dig her fingers in and drag him down to her and taste his sensual mouth again for herself. He caught her trembling hand in his and flashed her a shimmering smile of anticipation. 'If I touch you, I'll stay, but I believe that we should wait for our wedding night.'

Hot, chagrined colour flooded Ione's slanted cheek-bones. He spoke as though *she* had invited him to share her bed and her pride was as stung as her thoughts were in confusion. 'I—'

'Shush.' Brilliant golden eyes gleaming with very male satisfaction, he studied her as if she already belonged to him heart and soul and, smiling that heart-stopping smile, he rested a silencing fingertip against her parted lips. 'I'm flattered that you should be as eager as I am, but waiting always enhances the pleasure.'

As Alexio strode out of her bedroom Ione experienced a spasm of rage strong enough to deprive her of all breath and reason for several painful seconds. How *dared* he think that she would offer herself to him like some love-lorn, brainless wanton? How *dared* he assume that a momentary and slight desire to be kissed was the equivalent of an invitation to share her bed?

Alexio strolled back to his own suite at his leisure and smiled, thinking that marriage wasn't going to be so bad. Ione had been so deprived of freedom by her father that life with a tolerant and generous husband could only shine in comparison. He would not have to turn handstands to keep her content. And unless he was very much mistaken he had been blessed with a bride as hot-blooded as he was himself. Although he ached from the bite of a sexual restraint he was rarely forced to exercise, he was wholly confident that their wedding night would more than make up for that suffering...

CHAPTER FOUR

ON IONE'S wedding day eleven days later, a mysterious box wrapped in elegant gold paper was brought to her.

'Alexio's wedding gift.' Kalliope dealt her niece an impatient look. 'Well, open it up!'

Ione regarded the box with superstitious dread. She did not *want* to receive a present from the bridegroom whom she was planning to abandon within hours of their wedding! She had got nothing for him, had not even thought of an exchange of presents. Their marriage was only a cold-blooded business deal to be finalised in the church. Why was Alexio trying to personalise their relationship?

In exasperation, her aunt opened the box herself and lifted out an oval leather jewel case. Ione reached out in haste to take charge of the case. She flipped up the lid to expose a delicate emerald necklace adorned with fine diamond drops. It was exquisite but it meant nothing, she told herself. Alexio was simply going through the motions of what he believed was expected of him.

Kalliope frowned. 'Why that big box for that small case?'

Ione saw the edges of the tissue paper protruding from the carton and spread the paper back. Her heart missed a beat in shock when she saw the second gift. With reluctant hands, she lifted out the teddy bear that still bore the label of a world-famous auction house. He was a rare bear almost a hundred years old and he had a wonderfully expressive face. Her strained eyes misted with tears. Cosmas would have loved him.

'As if you needed another one of those things!' Kalliope exclaimed in astonished disappointment. 'Does your bridegroom think that you are still a little girl?'

Ione's brother had bought her teddy bears on his every trip abroad. After his death, she could not have made herself part with a single member of her collection for each and every one held a special memory of the big brother she had adored.

'Alexio would be well served if you took the toy to bed with you tonight instead of him!' Kalliope pronounced with earthy amusement. 'But he's clever and what a charmer he is. He knows how to touch a woman's heart. Who would credit that this marriage is only a business alliance arranged by your father?'

Face burning, Ione set the bear aside, struggling to regain her composure after that crack about sharing a bed with Alexio. That acid final comment from her aunt helped to speed up the process. Still tense as a bowstring, Ione looked in the mirror and twitched her short lace veil back into place. She had intended to allow Kalliope to choose her wedding dress. But when her aunt had demonstrated a desire to send her down the aisle weighted down with frills, bows and petticoats, she had changed her mind. After all, why *should* she appear before hundreds of people looking like a complete fright?

Her gown was a slender elegant sheath with a boat neckline and short sleeves and the very simplicity of cut flattered her diminutive height. Her wedding was a sham though, she reminded herself, and the gift of the bear merely proof that Alexio was worthy of his very bad reputation. Her chin came up. What womaniser had ever been successful without charm?

An hour later as the limo drew up outside the substantial church built by her father to celebrate her brother's birth almost thirty years earlier, Ione was no longer so sanguine. Her three bridesmaids were youthful distant cousins and virtual strangers to her. When the teenagers had expressed their surprise at the lack of the usual observances in advance of Ione's wedding, Kalliope had silenced them with an angry reproof. But the week before a Greek wedding *was* normally a social whirl of custom and fun experiences for the bride and her attendants. However, Minos Gakis had refused to allow his sister to fill the villa with female guests. Ione had been relieved, but she knew that her aunt had been very disappointed.

Sunlight gleaming over his proud dark head, Alexio was waiting on the church steps with a bouquet of flowers for her. Her heart hammered and her mouth ran dry. It was not a tradition she had expected him to observe and, immaculate in his well-cut dark suit, he looked spectacularly handsome. As she climbed out of the car his dark golden eyes raked over her with frank appreciation.

'Five minutes and counting,' Alexio teased under the voluble cover of the crowd of islanders calling out good wishes to them both. His keen gaze absorbing her taut pallor, he wondered if it was the prospect of the crammed church and the novelty of being the centre of attention that was making her so nervous.

It was a beautiful church and some of Ione's earliest memories were of her worship there as a child. Alexio's *koumbaros* or best man was his friend, Petros, and the other man carried out his duties with appropriate gravity. The service began with the elderly robed cleric blessing the exchange of rings and recognising their betrothal. Both bride and groom held a lit candle and Alexio linked his right hand with hers. Ione was trembling. With solemnity, they were crowned with orange blossom and then blessed by the priest. The timeless words of the ceremony roused her deepest and guiltiest misgivings.

As they sipped in turn from the wine that symbolised the sharing of all that life would bring, Alexio covered her hand with his, to steady her precarious hold on the cup. Ione was ghost-pale and she and her bridegroom circled the low table on which the bible rested and the guests showered them with rose petals and rice. The crowns removed, they were proclaimed man and wife.

'I thought you were about to faint,' Alexio breathed with visible concern as he urged her with all-male purpose through the crowds outside and straight into the limousine awaiting them. 'Are you all right?'

'I'm f-fine,' Ione stammered, fighting to suppress the uneasy feelings that had almost overpowered her during the service. What was done was done and there was no going back, she reasoned. Her hands knotted on her lap as she willed the driver to ferry them back to the villa at speed. The less time she spent alone with Alexio the happier she would be.

'You look very lovely,' Alexio commented.

'Thank you,' Ione muttered in a stifled voice.

'It's unfortunate that you couldn't meet my family before our wedding,' Alexio remarked. 'Is your father always so reluctant to entertain?'

'I'm afraid so.' Her father had no time for polite social courtesies and, as his sole interest in the Christoulakis family was Alexio, he wouldn't care if he had offended all of his son-in-law's relatives. She almost apologised on her parent's behalf until it occurred to her that, before very long, the Christoulakis family would have rather more embarrassing news with which to deal: her *desertion* of their son. Her heart sank and her tummy clenched.

When Alexio's parents and his sisters were the first to

approach her with warm smiles at the villa, Ione could not meet their eyes and did not know what she said in response to their friendly overtures. Her father signalled her from several feet away and, with a muttered apology, she hurried to his side.

Minos Gakis settled cold eyes on his daughter. 'You didn't smile once in the church. Make a better showing here before I lose patience with you.'

Just thinking that soon she would never have to cringe from such veiled threats again strengthened Ione. But an arm curved round her rigid spine and a rich, dark drawl sounded in her ear as Alexio murmured smooth as glass, 'But I have a lot of patience.'

Her father loosed a derisive bark of laughter. 'You'll need it, Ione may yet surprise you.'

At that crack, which Ione interpreted as a warning stab at the need to keep her illegitimate birth a secret, she coloured. As her father strode off Alexio's hold on her slight frame tightened and he looked down at her with pleated dark brows. 'Why is your father always so angry with you? What happened to create such a division between you?'

'We've just never been that close,' Ione muttered awkwardly, pained and embarrassed that he should question her on such a subject, for the strong bonds of affection between Alexio and his own family had been obvious even in the brief interaction she had witnessed.

Absorbing her downbent blonde head and her evasive manner, Alexio's brilliant eyes hardened. Why had Minos forecast that Ione might yet surprise him? Why was his bride acting as guilty as sin itself? It could only be something to do with the fisherman's son. That covert relationship was the most likely cause of the gulf between father and daughter. So why was she still dreaming about another man more than two years after the event?

Whatever, Alexio was already questioning his own protective and forgiving tolerance. She was a Gakis, he reminded himself. Any woman with the guts to defy Minos was no shrinking wallflower. Yet Ione had behaved throughout their wedding ceremony as though she were an early Christian martyr watching the bonfire being built.

During the luncheon that followed many speeches were made. Then came a lengthy performance from a famous singer and there was little opportunity for conversation between bride and groom. But by then even Ione had noticed the distinct chill that Alexio was exuding. Intelligence informed her that that was good, indeed even convenient in the circumstances, for it kept their interaction to the absolute minimum. Yet for some reason she could not content herself with that belief, could not prevent herself from sneaking anxious glances at him every chance she got and could not resist an inexplicable urgent need to rectify the situation.

'I never thanked you for the necklace...or the teddy bear,' Ione said uneasily half under her breath.

'Gratitude not required,' Alexio drawled.

'I didn't get anything for you...I didn't think,' Ione admitted, striving to understand why she had got into such a pointless dialogue and failing.

'I got you, didn't I?' Alexio countered with pronounced dryness.

As Ione glanced warily up at him, green eyes widening, the sheer strain stamped in her fragile features shook him. With a sharp pang of discomfiture, he remembered her telling him that she could be anything he wanted her to be. Only she wasn't accustomed to crowds and, thanks to her father's policy of keeping her at home, she knew hardly anybody. Yet, there was hardly a guest in the room who had not stared and stared at her simply because she was who she was: the Gakis heiress, whom precious few had seen before and even fewer knew anything about. Small wonder that she had been sick with nerves at the church and she needed reassurance, *not* censure.

Alexio closed his hand over her tense fingers and cradled them in his. 'This is a special day. Let's enjoy it,' he urged huskily.

His beautiful dark golden eyes connected with hers and her mind went blank as her breath caught in her throat. What he had said barely registered. She was conscious only of the warmth of his much larger hand engulfing hers and her own surge of relief that he had ditched his forbidding cool. Indeed, for a moment, she felt quite dizzy with the strength of that relief.

Alexio watched her pupils dilate, her cheeks blossom with colour and her lush pink mouth form into a tremulous smile, and felt like a very powerful magician. *Finally*, she was looking at him as a bride ought to look at her new husband. Almost imperceptibly she leant closer, her soft lips parting, and he released her hand to give a gentle teasing tug to the straying strand of pale blond hair brushing her cheekbone and waken her back to a sense of their surroundings.

'Later, *yineka mou*,' he promised huskily.

A split second after that, his best man, Petros, intervened. Grasping Ione's hand, the younger man urged her out of her seat and led her out onto the dance floor. There she hovered, staring back at Alexio while Petros marshalled guests into forming two circles around her. As the efficient Petros started off the dancing by signalling the band, traditional music filled the room and those in the circle got down on one knee to begin clapping. Still mesmerised by Alexio's eyes, Ione was more aware of the rapid thunder of her own heartbeat and a bubbling, unfamiliar sense of lightheartedness.

Alexio rose in one lithe motion, clapping in time with the music. He really *was* so beautiful he made her ache, she conceded helplessly, her bright gaze welded to his lean, strong features. In fact every time she looked at Alexio, he seemed to get more gorgeous, and he had been more generous in response to her awkward behaviour. But then how could he know *why* she had been so silent and strained? As her conscience again threatened her composure she locked it out and found it simplest just to watch Alexio.

When the last of the guests had completed the obligatory circling of the bride, Alexio folded Ione into his arms to dance. Kalliope smashed a plate on the floor, encouraging those at the top table to follow suit. Alexio winced at the racket, caught an amusing glimpse of his refined mother forcing herself to follow Kalliope's lead and laughed. '*Very* traditional.'

Ione turned her blushing face into a wide shoulder, for the smashing of crockery signified good luck, happiness and the permanence of marriage.

'While everybody is otherwise engaged...' Alexio curved a purposeful hand to the nape of her neck to tip back her head.

'Yes?' Ione met his smouldering golden scrutiny. Her mouth ran dry and she tensed. Suddenly the exuberant raised voices and the noise of breaking crockery receded from her awareness, leaving only the racing thump of her own heartbeat thrumming in her ears.

'I want to kiss my bride...' Alexio imparted, whirling her in one dexterous move behind one of the pillars in the grand ballroom and pressing her back against it.

Excitement claimed Ione even before he touched her. A wild leap of longing thrilled through her as he spread her back against the unyielding stone surface. He was all masculine mastery and cool but for the flare of hunger in his brilliant eyes. Arching her spine, tilting her head back was instinctive.

'...and my bride wants to kiss me,' Alexio savoured with lancing satisfaction, claiming her parted lips with a hot, urgent immediacy that took her breath away and sent her senses spinning.

The plunge of his tongue inside the sensitive interior of her mouth made her cling to him, dig her fingers into his broad shoulders and tremble. Her whole body felt hot and tight and charged. His sexual intensity electrified her. A flame fired low in her pelvis and the resulting rise of need provoked a stifled moan from her. She pushed forward into him, automatically seeking closer connection with his big, powerful frame. In a sudden movement, he was there, one hard hand curving to her hips to urge her into contact with his potent arousal while the forceful demand of his mouth sent her head back against the wall. Her senses sang, exhilarated by the raw, masculine strength and feel of him, the explosive hunger that answered her own.

When Alexio jerked back from her with a muttered curse word, dark colour scored his hard cheekbones and his molten gaze flared into hers only for a split second. She was pale, visibly shaken, wide eyes evading his and veiling. Alexio was so furious with himself that he almost punched the wall in frustration. Pinning his tiny virginal bride to a pillar and coming on to her as if he wanted to take her on the spot was downright crude. But when her lush, soft mouth had opened under his with such shy invitation, the force of his own hunger had almost overwhelmed him.

'I'm sorry,' he said flatly. 'Did I hurt you?'

Ione was so ashamed of herself, she couldn't even look him in the face. She shook her head in answer and she wanted to sink through the floor. *He* had pulled back from *her*, probably in surprise at the wanton way she had urged him on in a public place. It wasn't his fault. Men were useless at resisting temptation, which was why women were supposed to stay in control, Ione thought, cringing over her own behaviour. Pure lust had grabbed her and swept her away.

'Excuse me...' she framed in a mortified whisper and fled.

Assailed by all the stark annoyance of a male who prided himself on his every move around her sex, Alexio gave vent to his feelings and punched the wall. Flexing his bruised knuckles in the aftermath, he glanced up to see his father poised only feet away.

Sander Christoulakis spread rueful, expressive hands and grimaced. 'I know I shouldn't interfere...'

Then don't. Alexio ground his teeth together in outraged silence.

'But Ione's a shy little thing, *not* the kind of woman you're used to,' Sander pronounced in a tone of reproach. 'Treat her with respect.'

Ione headed for the library, which was one of her favourite retreats, but she hesitated outside the ajar door when she heard voices within.

'Ione's so drab...poor Alexio!' a youthful female voice was lamenting. 'This marriage is a tragedy. I bet my brother thinks he's never going to fall in love again after Crystal but he'll be bored and miserable with Ione and he'll end up taking a mistress.'

'Knowing your brother, probably *more* than one!' her

companion giggled. 'Do you realise that I've seen at least four women here that are exes of his?'

Alexio's kid sister, Delphia, was the first speaker and the other girl probably one of her pals. Ione remembered her aunt enquiring after Alexio's youngest sister. His fifteen-year-old sibling had been a late-born surprise when he and his other sister had been in their teens. He had smiled and confessed that Delphia was spoilt rotten by all of them. Ione had wondered then what it felt like to be spoilt rotten.

Drab? Well, she thought wryly, on a day when she was so much on show there had been good reason for her to maintain her usual unadventurous appearance. But that evening for the first time she would be stepping out wearing fashionable clothes and she was pretty sure that even a best friend, had she been allowed to retain one, wouldn't recognise her as Ione Gakis.

As for what Delphia had forecast? Out of the mouths of babes, Ione reflected with pained cynicism. Were she to stay married to Alexio, he would inevitably stray in search of more exciting conquests and she would be expected to turn a blind eye to his infidelity and be grateful for what small share she had of his attention. As long as he was discreet, as long as he did not divorce her and break up their family, few would think the worse of him for betraying her. She knew the rules of their society and it was still very much a man's world. Hadn't she grown up watching her mother pretend ignorance of her father's extra-marital forays?

What on earth had come over her during the past hour? With hindsight, she was aghast at her own weak-minded foolishness. All Alexio had had to do was reach for her hand and there she had been hanging on his every word and gazing at him as though he had just stepped down from heaven to grace her with his presence! She had even been dumb enough to get a sexual thrill out of being flattened against a pillar like some willing tart in a dark doorway. She lashed herself with that image. She had acted like an idiot.

Yet what might their marriage have been like had he *loved* her? That thought crept in, rebelling against her need to stifle it. But then what did a male like Alexio Christoulakis really *know* about love? Women had always fallen at his feet in large numbers.

Crystal Denby had been a sexy, provocative challenge, a tease and a flirt, who had played him at his own game until he'd finally given her an engagement ring. But had Crystal survived, would he ever actually have got around to *marrying* her? For Alexio was so essentially Greek. In his heart he really wanted to marry a virgin. And in a few hours' time, he would also expect his bride to spread herself happily across the marital bed even though she barely knew him. A sensitive guy? Throw her a teddy bear and jump her. About as sensitive as concrete laced with steel.

Although the reception would go on into the early hours of the morning, Ione went off to get changed. Her maid had laid out a green dress and jacket, the essential suit chosen by Kalliope, and Ione removed her wedding gown and put in on. Her heartbeat speeded up as she went into the dressing room to lift out the small attaché case stowed at the back of one of the wardrobes.

In the act of leaving her bedroom, she paused and glanced back at the forlorn teddy bear abandoned on the bed. The bear Alexio had given her. His name was Edward. It had said so on his label and he was an English bear, so didn't he deserve to go home to England with her? Biting her lip in indecision, she studied the rest of her bear collection and then hurried over to the bed, unlocked the attaché case and squashed Edward in.

Alexio watched his bride come down the main staircase. The suit was out of the ark in design but the shade enhanced her delicate colouring and nothing could conceal the grace of her slender figure. His whole body tensed on the hard, heavy rise of desire and raw exasperation flashed through him. What was it about her? Or was it the perverse knowledge that she was *his* now, his in a way that no other woman had ever been? He only knew that she excited him more than any woman had in a long time.

And he couldn't wait to take her shopping in Paris. A faint smile played over his wide, sensual mouth. He was already picturing the innocent pleasure she would find in a whole host of things that he and all the women he had ever known took for granted. He strode forward to greet her, but her aunt and her father and a vociferous clutch of guests demanded her attention.

Within twenty minutes they were boarding the helicopter that would drop them off at the airport. In a sudden movement, Ione turned back to Alexio, her profile taut. 'Will you ask the pilot to fly over the island first?'

'If that's what you want.' Alexio was surprised. Having witnessed enough throughout the day to confirm his suspicion that Ione appeared to rate little higher than the domestic staff in the eyes of her father and her aunt, he had somehow assumed that she would leave the island without a backward glance. He was too much of a cynic, he told himself. Naturally she was attached to her family.

As the pilot flew over Lexos, Ione gazed down at her home. Now that it would no longer be her prison, she could think of it as her home again and recall the good memories that in more recent years she had almost forgotten. She was leaving everything she possessed behind and she knew she would never see any of it again. Her father would never forgive her. He would have no need to do so with Alexio as his son-in-law.

'I hope you like my house in Paris,' Alexio remarked as they walked towards his private jet at the airport. 'It's…unusual.'

'I saw a magazine article on it once.' Had Ione's nerves not been jumping like electrified beans by that stage, she might have smiled at his selection of that particular word. In that magazine spread, Crystal Denby had been arranged on a sofa shaped like a giant pair of scarlet lips. There had been jazzy purple wallpaper in the background, an animal skin fur at her feet and enormous gilded blackamoor torcheres burning to either side of her. A quite unforgettable image of the sex kitten at home, Ione conceded. He had allowed his former fiancée to turn a gracious seventeenth century townhouse into the tasteless and showy equivalent of a bordello.

'Are you always this quiet?' Alexio enquired when the jet was airborne.

Ione pretended to stifle a yawn and sighed. 'I'm sorry…I'm so sleepy.'

When she appeared to drift off to sleep within minutes, Alexio resisted an ungenerous urge to shake her awake again. It *had* been a long day for her. Things could only get better; well, they could hardly get worse. He had almost forgotten what her voice sounded like. She shied away from his smallest touch and her beautiful eyes would not meet his. Possibly he deserved that, but it seemed to him that the young woman who had touched him with her confession that she wanted to marry him more than anything else in the world had suffered a distinct change of heart. And Alexio, who had never in his thirty years of existence had to make an effort to hold the attention of a woman, really didn't know how to handle that.

As Ione climbed out of the limo outside the Paris townhouse, she was so pale and tense that Alexio was afraid that a sudden movement might shatter her to pieces like glass.

'Are you feeling OK?' Alexio was amazed at how keen he was to hear that she was feeling dreadful. Illness he could cope with. Illness would explain everything.

'G-great…' Ione stammered like a schoolgirl, gripping her little case with tense fingers.

Alexio took a deep breath and lifted her off her feet into his arms. She loosed a startled cry as if she were under attack and strained green eyes finally met his in a head-on collision as he looked down at her. 'What are you doing?'

'Carrying you over the threshold.'

'Why…why are you doing that?' Ione gasped, clutching her case from beneath the lid of which Alexio could now see an edge of tartan ribbon protruding. Edward's ribbon. Out of all the rest of those bears, she had brought *his* gift with her. At a moment when he was in need of encouragement, it was a welcome revelation.

'It's an English custom. Your mother was English,' Alexio murmured gently.

The mere mention of England was sufficient to paralyse Ione. Both her natural mother and her adoptive mother might have been English, but all Ione could think about was the reality that she was planning to run off to London that same evening. As her colour fluctuated and her eyes veiled Alexio surveyed her with a questioning look.

He set her down in a spacious hall. A magnificent art

deco table sat in the centre, embellished with a glorious arrangement of white lilies.

'I believe the staff are ready to serve dinner.' Alexio cast open the door of a dining room furnished in similar style.

At even the mention of food, Ione's tummy churned. She had little more than two and a half hours left in which to get back to the airport.

'I'd like to freshen up,' she said tightly, unable to bring herself to look at him.

Alexio took her upstairs and showed her into the master bedroom suite. With a decor of dull gold and green and traditional furniture, it stood out like a major statement from what she had so far seen of the rest of the house. Ione understood. Since Crystal's death, he had had it redecorated.

'I'll leave you…' But Alexio hovered and reached without warning for her clenched hands, forcing her to let go of the small case. '*Look* at me…'

'That's better,' he said.

Her mouth running dry, she connected with brilliant dark golden eyes and trembled. Her surging emotions threatened her superficial hold on her composure. He released one hand to brush a fine strand of blonde hair back from her brow. His long brown fingers surprisingly gentle. At the touch of him, a frisson of piercing awareness gripped Ione and her legs wobbled. Her nostrils flared on the already familiar male scent of him: husky and warm overlaid with a faint hint of some aromatic lotion.

She wanted more. Standing there quivering at that moment, she knew she wanted him as she had not known she could want any man. For she wanted Alexio against all reason, caution and self-preservation. Her nipples were swollen, sensitive buds pushing against the cups of her bra, and at the heart of her she was liquid with longing. Shame swept over her, shame that he could already have that much power over her.

He kissed her long and slow and deep and it was an entire banquet of sweet, sensual sensation. The stroke of his tongue within her mouth was unbearably exciting. The reality that no other part of their bodies touched only heightened her craving for the hard muscularity of him against her softer curves. Low in her throat, she heard herself moan, for the hunger tearing at her grew more powerful with every subtle movement of his sensual mouth on hers.

'I'll see you downstairs.' Freeing her, Alexio stepped back, hard cheekbones taut, smouldering golden eyes burning over the feverish flush on her triangular face with blatant male appreciation.

She moved back with unsteady abruptness and her shoulder blades met the solid wall and took support from it. She didn't want him to go. She wanted him to stay. Shock and fear of the unknown person that had surfaced inside her held her rigid. She stared at him, mesmerised by his lean, hard features; the play of light and shadow over his stunning eyes and chiseled cheekbones, the hard strength and command stamped into every angular line of his bronzed face.

Dragging her attention from him almost physically hurt and it took every ounce of her will-power. She deserved *better* than such a marriage, she reasoned in a frantic, feverish argument with herself. She deserved to be more than part of a callous business deal. And if she stayed, if she surrendered to the weak and dangerous promptings of her own heart, she would fall in love with Alexio Christoulakis and any hope of living her own life and any real prospect of finding happiness would be at an end.

She was a naive pushover for a male as sophisticated and sexually intense as Alexio. But that was only because she had no true experience of other men. Her sad little flirtation with Yannis scarcely counted. In fact, what she was suffering from now was probably no more than an intoxicating rush of physical curiosity and too many hormones in her bloodstream.

What she could not afford to forget was the *kind* of male Alexio was. A powerful Greek tycoon, who by their marriage would become all the more powerful. He had already acquired a name for ruthlessness that had been sufficient to impress her father. He would be no less ruthless when it came to his private life. For only a little while would she be a novelty, for she did not have what it would take to hold such a man. Neither the traffic-stopping beauty, nor the adventurous personality, not even the sexual expertise that would grip his attention for longer. If she stayed with Alexio, he would destroy her as surely as her father had destroyed her mother.

Her strength of purpose recaptured, Ione slipped out of the room to search for the most promising exit from the townhouse. After a nerve-racking exploration of the upper two floors she came back to the master suite in despair and only then discovered that a fire escape ran from the bathroom window down to an alleyway far below. Locking the door, she stripped and changed into the outfit in her attaché case. She left the note she had prepared. The transformation she achieved was done at speed, for she knew that she had little time left before either Alexio or one of the staff came to remind her about dinner.

Her heart was literally in her mouth as she opened the window, turned her back on the drop that terrified her out of her wits and climbed out. Her legs dangled before her feet finally connected with the small wrought-iron platform below the sill. She felt with damp palms for the balustrade. Rigid with fear, she descended the metal steps, edging round each landing to the next level while struggling to see where she was going without looking down. On solid ground again, she staggered and then, even though her legs were still shaking and she felt sick as a dog with nerves and fright, she forced herself to run.

Alexio was on the brink of going upstairs when Tipo, the burly head of Ione's protection team, appeared in the hall and rushed past him to head up there himself.

Minos had insisted that Ione would be at risk without round-the-clock protection. Alexio had considered four security men a quite excessive number for such a task until his father-in-law had admitted that he had had recent serious threats made against him. Well aware of how many enemies the older man had, Alexio had realised that his bride might indeed be in danger. On their honeymoon, she would be much more accessible than her parent on his private island.

'Where are you going?' Alexio was annoyed that his decree that the bodyguards must remain unobtrusive was already being disregarded. After all, what possible harm could come to Ione in his home while he was present?

'A window alarm went off up here!' the thickset older man called back and he was already talking into his handset to the rest of his team.

His lean, powerful face set in thunderous lines, Alexio reached the top landing in a couple of strides and went straight into the master bedroom where he expected to find that Ione had fallen asleep on the bed. Seeing the bathroom door closed instead, he knocked on it, outraged at the hue and cry being roused and the invasion of their privacy.

That fool of a man might have burst into the room while Ione was undressing!

'I'll break the door down,' Tipo offered.

'Ione?' Ignoring the bodyguard, Alexio rapped on the door a second time and then, motivated by genuine concern that his wife might have gone to sleep in the bath, he put a big shoulder to the solid wood and forced the lock.

'She's done a runner.' Drawing level with Alexio, Tipo scowled at the open window and the discarded garments lying on the floor.

'I beg your pardon?' Alexio breathed.

'She'll be at the airport. We'll bring her back,' his companion informed him and walked away.

For the space of a minute, Alexio was in total disbelieving shock, but during that minute he was anything but inactive. He strode through every bedroom and shouted Ione's name over the bannister in case she was downstairs in one of the other reception rooms. He could not credit the concept that she had vanished. Momentarily, his mind refused to accept what struck him as an impossibility. But his next thought was that someone could have come up that fire escape and kidnapped her! Sick at the tide of threatening images bombarding him, Alexio raced back to the *en suite* bathroom to study it again.

This time he noticed the sheet of paper wedged by one corner beneath the mirror. Even from the doorway he was able to read it.

'I'm sorry but I couldn't stay. Ione.'

Not a ransom note? A note from Ione herself. Alexio stared at it with fixed attention, striving to dig something out of that single sentence that might make the remotest sense to him. He reached the hall again in five seconds flat. Tipo was already barrelling out the front door.

'What the hell is going on?' Alexio demanded.

'You can trust us to handle this. Mr Gakis would like you to call him.'

At that suggestion, Alexio might have said something very short and succinct had he not been too preoccupied to waste the time. His bride had walked out on him...*why*? An image of her white, scared face flashed into his mind. Throughout the day, Ione had been a bag of nerves and evidently she had been a lot more distressed than he had appreciated.

Tipo cleared his throat. 'Mr Gakis wants us to fly his daughter home to the island where he can look after her.'

Raw outrage flashed through Alexio's lean, taut length with energising force. 'My wife is a Christoulakis and *I* will look after her!'

Three minutes later, Alexio climbed into his sports car. Determined to reach the airport in advance of Tipo and his bully boys, he used every short cut he knew. He was on automatic pilot because on one level he still could not accept that Ione could have done something so outrageous as leave him before the ink was even dry on their marriage licence. She had been scared. What of? *Him?* An incredulous laugh of dismissal started in his throat and then died there as he recalled the manner in which she had run from him earlier in the day.

He had had the dim idea that terrified virgins died out along with long skirts and clothed piano legs but Ione had had a rather strange upbringing, he acknowledged, striving to understand the incomprehensible. And then it dawned on him that Ione might have fled because she was *not* the wholly inexperienced bride he had been led to expect and that she might be afraid that her bridegroom would create hell over that discovery. As he mulled over what he had already learned about the fisherman's son Alexio's hard profile took on a forbidding cast. He reckoned a *lack* of virginity was the more likely possibility.

His brilliant dark eyes were grim. So he was disappointed, but he was also appalled that the matter could have assumed such proportions in Ione's mind that the only solution she could see was walking out on their marriage. An unpleasant recollection of Ione quailing beneath the threat of her angry father's fist assailed him at that point. Fear of her bridegroom's reaction might well have had sufficient power to make his bride bolt. How was she to *know* that he wasn't like her father?

In spite of her success in making it to the airport and purchasing her ticket, an increasing sense of bewildering misery and uncertainty was weighing on Ione.

The flight to London was delayed but, although she could have gone through the gates to wait in greater security and privacy, she had not yet been able to make herself take that final step. Having assumed that airports were very anonymous places, she was intimidated by the manner in which people seemed to be staring at her. Maybe she just looked odd. Maybe people could see how nervous and unhappy she was and were wondering what was the matter with her. It wasn't important, she told herself. Soon she would be in England and that much closer to finding her sister, Misty. Unfortunately that reflection did not bring the comfort she had believed it would.

What must Alexio think of her? That was all Ione could *really* think about: how Alexio must be feeling. He had to have found out by now that she had gone. He would not understand why she had disappeared. How could he? He would simply think that she was crazy. Would he feel hurt? His pride would certainly be hurt. He would curse the day he had first met her, for in no way did he deserve the shame and embarrassment her vanishing act would bring down on the Christoulakis family.

Alexio strode through the airport like a man on a mission. He checked the flight schedule. There was a flight to Greece in two hours. But *would* Ione go home to her irate parent? If not, where else would she go? She had had no close friends at their wedding. And then he recalled her discomfited reaction to his teasing reminder that her mother had been English. Of course, England. Surely she had to have some relatives there? The London flight had been due to take off in an hour but it was running late. He breathed a little easier.

Alexio saw Edward the bear before he recognized his wife. Her back turned to him, a young girl who looked like a teenager was gazing into a shop with a bear who might have been Edward's double tucked beneath her arm. Alexio stilled, his gaze welding to the glorious fall of platinum fair hair falling to the girl's waist. Ione? Could it be? In a chequer-board print skirt so tiny she should have been arrested for wearing it? Not to mention a pink crop top that exposed her bare midriff and absurd shoes with heels studded with stones that glittered?

Ione? Alexio was stunned, incredulous and awake to the reality that there was not a man within fifty yards failing to pay heed to her. He watched her stroll on to a magazine display and the slow, gliding walk was pure sex and Ione to the hilt. He saw her full face and snatched in a startled breath. The madonna perfection had been enhanced with cosmetics. She looked bloody spectacular, Alexio thought with a sudden stab of fury. He watched his wife produce an entire handful of high denomination currency to buy one little magazine. The guy on the stand was so entranced by the fairy-tale princess before him that he started to explain what the notes were.

A shy little thing, Sander had called her…

Having stuffed all the notes back into her miniature handbag as she moved away from the stand, Ione glanced up. When she saw Alexio, devastated disbelief stopped her in her tracks, for she could not imagine how he could have found her. He was only twenty feet away: very tall and dark and powerful, lean, strong face hard. Even before she clashed with his glittering golden gaze, her chest tightened and breathing became a severe challenge.

'What…w-what are you doing here?' she heard herself stammer foolishly.

'You are my wife,' Alexio breathed in a roughened undertone that was not quite steady.

And with those four words, he faced Ione with a reality that she had done virtually everything to avoid acknowledging. In the space of an instant, she was cast back to the outset of the day and the sombre and beautiful church service. For the first time an honest appreciation of what she had done crept up out of Ione's subconscious and overwhelmed her: she *had* married him.

In fact she had done even worse than that, her conscience told her. She had gone to great lengths to persuade Alexio that she could hardly wait to become his wife. In short, she had met his sincerity with deception and his honesty with evasion and lies. Ione, who had always prided herself on her moral values, was shattered by that belated reappraisal of her own behaviour.

'I don't know that to say…'

Alexio had plenty to say but sufficient self-control to know that a busy airport was not the place in which to give vent to his feelings. As to what those feelings were, he had not the slightest idea, for blistering anger had superseded all else. He closed a powerful hand to her wrist.

'You will explain yourself to me and then I will decide what *I* want to do.'

'Alexio…I—'

'Not a word until we have privacy,' Alexio grated with an explosive edge of his dark, deep voice.

Intercepting a poleaxed glance from a passing business-man lusting over his bride's scantily clad body, Alexio glowered at the offender in a righteous rage. Only narrowly overcoming an urge to remove his suit jacket and wrap Ione in it, he herded her into the nearest fashion shop instead.

Ione stood like a wooden image while Alexio swept a coat from the display and tossed it on the counter with a credit card. She was in shock. What on earth was he doing? And why was she letting him take control? He was her husband and as such deserving of a great deal more consideration than she had so far shown him. The guilt she was experiencing was now being followed by the strangest sensation of relief and acceptance.

The security tag removed, Alexio retrieved the coat and extended it to her. Embarrassed by the wide-eyed curiosity of the sales assistant, Ione dug reluctant arms into the sleeves. The raincoat was far too long for her and almost reached her ankles. But Alexio bent down and buttoned the coat right down to the last button in case it fell open.

'Why…?' Ione finally voiced her complete bewilder-ment.

'While you carry my name, you will not parade around in public dressed like a baby hooker!' Alexio informed her in a raw undertone in Greek, the vague suspicion that he might be overreacting stifled entirely by the fierce satis-faction he gained from covering every visible inch of her slender curves from the attention of other men.

Hot, mortified colour drenched Ione's pallor. A baby

hooker? How dare he? She was dressed in the height of fashion. He was just being cruel. But he was also betraying the exact same incredulous fury that her father would have exhibited had he seen her got up in such an outfit. She discovered at that moment that she could not keep a single thought in her head for longer than ten seconds. The sheer shock value of finally admitting to herself that Alexio Christoulakis was her husband seemed to have paralysed her brain cells.

He would take her to an airport hotel to talk, Alexio decided. Whatever happened, whatever she confessed, he would *not* lose his temper. But his intelligence was already drawing up scenarios that made him feel angrier than ever. Had he been a complete dupe? Was she *still* in love with the fisherman's son? What else was he to think when he found her at the airport dressed to kill and in no way resembling the shy and modest bride he had married? Had she run away to meet up with that bastard, Yannis, somewhere? On her terms had their marriage merely been an escape route from a domineering father determined to prevent her from being with a man of whom he disapproved?

CHAPTER FIVE

ONLY fifteen minutes later, Ione found herself standing in the centre of a large and luxurious hotel suite still clutching Edward, her bag and her attaché case.

'I want only the truth,' Alexio delivered with as near an approximation of level diction as he could manage, his lean, powerful frame rigid with tension as he awaited her explanation.

Ione gazed at him with a fast-beating heart, her attention roaming over his lean, dark, devastating face and the marks of strain there before going into guilty retreat. Her conscience almost slaughtered her. How could she tell him such a terrible truth? If he knew how utterly selfish and dishonest she had been he would never, ever forgive her. He would despise her for rewarding his integrity and trust with a tissue of unscrupulous lies and pretences. And it was only then, when she looked up and collided afresh with his scorching golden eyes, that she realised that she could not *bear* the idea of Alexio turning away from her in complete disgust. That second shattering piece of self-revelation shook her to her very depths.

In the humming silence, Alexio drew in a stark sustaining breath. 'Why don't you take your coat off?'

'I—'

'I'm your husband,' Alexio purred as he strode forward. Removing the bear and the bags from her, he tossed them aside. 'If a sudden attack of modesty didn't get to you in public, why should you shrink from displaying yourself to me?'

Ione was paralysed to the spot as lean, deft fingers dealt summarily with the buttons of her coat. Her frantic thoughts had gone into free fall when she'd registered that her biggest fear now was that Alexio would walk away. But her brain and her tongue would not unite, for registering that Alexio had mystifyingly become more important to her than her quest for her own sister and freedom filled her with stricken and genuine bewilderment. 'You said I looked like a baby hooker—'

'I was too kind.' Alexio flung the coat aside and stepped back to let his shimmering scrutiny wander at a leisurely pace over her.

Ione tensed even more beneath the surprising discovery that, when Alexio looked at her in that certain indefinable way, she felt half naked and horribly self-conscious. As his insolent appraisal rested on the upswell of her breasts, her nipples pinched tight and butterflies broke loose in her quivering tummy. He raked his scrutiny down to her sleek bare midriff and the tight little skirt that merely accentuated her slender shapely length of leg. He forced his attention back up again to her exquisite face, his big, powerful body taut and throbbing with sudden fierce but furious sexual hunger.

Inflamed with squirming discomfiture by that intimate reconnaissance of her figure, Ione felt like a slave on the block. She could hardly breathe and her heart was banging up against her breastbone in panic. Yet she could not dredge her dilated eyes from him or control the frisson of disturbing heat curling up from low in her pelvis.

'Silence doesn't become you in that outfit,' Alexio drawled with cutting candour. 'So, assuming that you weren't cruising in search of an illicit sexual thrill from a complete stranger on our wedding night…where *were* you going and why?'

Ione had no idea what to say, for she had already recognised that the truth was beyond the bounds of all forgiveness. 'I don't know…'

'You don't know,' Alexio repeated as he prowled round the room like a lion ready to spring and then he flung back his proud dark head, fixed her with eyes as hard as granite and roared. 'What sort of an answer is that? This morning we got married…this evening you sneaked down a fire escape, got tarted up like a streetwalker and raced for the airport! Now either you are in severe need of therapy or you had a good reason for doing that!'

'I was going to fly to London.'

Alexio froze at that confirmation and marvelled at his own incredible reluctance to accept the obvious. His strong jawline clenched. Had he thought she had fled to the airport simply to watch big aeroplanes land?

'How did Tipo know that you would be at the airport?' he demanded.

Ione gave him a shaken look. 'Tipo is *here*…in Paris?'

Alexio watched her pallor grow. Clear as day, he saw her fear at the mere mention of the older man's name, but his anger only hardened when he recognised his own instinctive stab of concern that that should be the case.

'I thought we were on our own here…' A weak little laugh fell from Ione's dry mouth as her tummy somersaulted on a mental image of the treatment she would have received had her father's henchmen found her first.

'I called you my wife but a woman who walks out within hours of taking her wedding vows is *no* wife of mine,' Alexio framed with biting clarity. 'However, I have a right to know *who* you were planning to meet!'

'Meet?' Ione gave him a blank look, her mind still endeavouring to cope with that first grim statement. Of course, he did not want such a wife. No man would want such a wife. A wife without loyalty, decency or honesty. She cringed. What else could she expect? She had burnt her boats. A hollow shell-shocked feeling began to engulf her in the wake of that acceptance. She was still free, she tried to tell herself. Not being as naive as she had been at eighteen, she knew that her bodyguards could not force her to go anywhere against her will if she was ready to fight back with the threat of a public scene that might reach the newspapers. But somehow that reality was of little consolation.

'The truth!' Alexio thundered back at her in explosive frustration. 'I want the truth. Who is waiting to meet you in London?'

'No one…no one even knows I was going there,' Ione muttered, failing to catch his drift.

'Not even Yannis…?' Alexio prompted in a dark-timbred drawl that fairly bristled with incipient threat.

'Yannis?' Ione parroted in confusion. 'Why would I be meeting with Yannis after all this time? I don't even know where he lives.'

The silence hung there like a sheet of glass waiting to crash.

Still seething with brooding suspicion, Alexio studied her. All trust was gone. He had not thought her capable of what she had already done. Every time he took in another appraisal of her startlingly provocative appearance, he became more incensed. 'Ione may yet surprise you,' Minos had quipped. And Ione had. But Alexio would allow no woman to make a fool of him.

'If there's not another man involved, why were you heading for London?' Like a perfect living doll, he reflected, rating the fabulous hair, the stunning face, the delicate but shapely curves and perfect legs. Every guy's fantasy right down to the innocent look of anxious appeal in her huge green eyes. Only a bride who did a runner on their wedding night was not *his* fantasy.

'Of course there's not another man involved!' Ione was shocked that he could suspect her of such a thing and then flung into deeper shock by the recollection that she *had* been planning on finding a boyfriend, who kissed as he did. As if men were interchangeable objects and one was as good as another. As if their marriage and her vows of fidelity had meant nothing to her. And too late, Ione was discovering that she was not as fearlessly unconventional nor as single-minded as she had believed she could be. At least not when it came to the prospect of for ever saying goodbye to Alexio Christoulakis.

'There is nothing more to say.' Lean, powerful face set in rigid forbidding lines, Alexio surveyed her with stormy golden eyes, for, even though he was willing to accept that no third party had precipitated her departure, he could not overlook what she had done or avoid interpreting it. 'It's clear to me that you had second thoughts about our marriage even before you got to the church. You would have saved us both a great deal of embarrassment had you had the courage to admit that then.'

Tears of bitter regret stung Ione's shaken eyes and she gulped back the painful ache in her throat. She had been so stubborn, so set on protecting herself and thinking the very worst of him that she had deceived herself right up until the last possible moment. She hadn't gone through the gates to await her flight, for getting out of there again without creating a huge fuss would have been a challenge. She had hung around restive and indecisive, fighting her own turmoil, refusing to admit even to herself that she didn't actually *want* to leave Alexio. She had behaved like a stupid child and what she was getting now was her just deserts because *he* wasn't a child, he was an adult.

'I thought I wanted to be free…' Ione explained half under her breath. 'I've never been free. Until tonight when I left this house, I have never been anywhere alone in my whole life.'

Alexio was taut, still, silent, but his gaze was lodged to her lovely green eyes and incredible eyelashes. When she blinked those long, dark lashes almost hit her cheekbones.

'I thought the worst of you…I panicked,' Ione confided in a breathless appeal. 'But I didn't think through what I was doing.'

At that moment, thinking was not uppermost in Alexio's mind either, but a word like 'panic' did dovetail beautifully with his earlier suspicion that his bride had bolted because she was a more delicate flower than he in his crude masculine insensitivity had appreciated. While his ferocious anger drained away at remarkable speed, his attention extended to take in the lush, moist pink of her mouth and he tensed in exquisite physical discomfort while at the same time assuring himself that no woman had ever got round him with eyes the colour of emeralds and soft, persuasive words.

'Do you think…do you think you could give me another chance?' Ione whispered, cringing for herself even as she voiced that plea, but knowing in her heart that she had no choice. He was Greek and she had injured his pride. Compromise wasn't his style. If he walked out, he was never, ever coming back.

Rationally, Alexio thought that might be possible with perhaps ten new security men on constant alert. She was a little wired. There was no escaping that conclusion. Any woman who had to go down a fire escape and get as far as the airport before she could recognise that she wanted to stay married to him was…? Sensitive, fragile and needed careful handling. And a word about not lugging

Edward the bear about in public might not go amiss. Not to mention the danger of wearing extraordinary shoes encrusted with what he suspected were genuine diamonds and flourishing enormous sums of money at news stands.

'Alexio…?'

'I'll think about it,' Alexio drawled with husky superiority.

Flames of discomfited colour lit Ione's face at that ungenerous response.

'It's more than you deserve, *yineka mou*,' Alexio informed her, brilliant dark golden eyes striking hers in unashamed challenge. 'You still have a lot of growing up to do. So persuade me to reconsider my options.'

Her soft mouth compressed, her eyes flaring before she hastily veiled them, outraged by that comeback but biting her tongue. She could not understand her own desire to fight with him. She never fought with anyone. Her battles had always been by necessity more subtle. His mobile phone shrilled. He switched it off. The silence came back humming with seething tension and the nape of her neck tingled until she lifted her head again.

'I don't like silence…I don't like sulks.' Alexio surveyed her steadily and stretched out his hands. 'Come here…'

And Ione didn't like that either. In fact, being ordered around was exactly what she hated most, but when Alexio fixed those expectant dark golden eyes on her it was as if her backbone and her pride went into retreat. She was just so shaken up by what had happened and still in so much turmoil, for she had yet to work out when and how he had contrived to steal her brain from her body and leave her feeling that no other man could replace him. That was nonsense, total nonsense and she loathed herself, but her feet moved even though she tried to will them into paralysis and that terrible, helpless craving for him streaked through her like a banner of shame.

'Naturally, I want to make love to you,' Alexio confessed in a roughened undertone. 'If you don't want that, go now because I can't live with a wife who shrinks from me.'

Ione reddened. 'I'm not going to shrink!'

Alexio dealt her a wolfish smile that sent her pulses crazy. 'I don't need a virgin bride either. I might have liked the experience just once. What Greek male could say otherwise? But I can live without it and think no less of you than I do of myself. Marriage lasts a lot longer than the wedding night, *yineka mou*.'

He lost Ione there, for she could not credit that he could be seriously suggesting that she had had other lovers. But she was too wary to question him lest she fall into some trap of the manipulative verbal variety at which her own father excelled. In any case, she was far too taken up with the quivering inner heat of her own body because, barely twelve inches from Alexio's big, powerful frame, anything more mentally strenuous demanded too much of her. He just smiled and deep down inside her somewhere it was as though her very bones were melting.

'The first time I saw you…*really* saw you, you came into my room with the linen to change the bed.' Alexio drew her up against him, molten golden eyes roving over her with heated appreciation. 'I burned for you then. You looked so wholesome that you were a walking temptation. I imagined peeling you out of that shapeless dark dress that I mistook for a uniform and laying you down on that bed—'

Ione was listening to him with hot cheeks and wide, doubting eyes. 'No…you hardly looked at me—'

'You were too busy trying to achieve hospital corners

on the bed to notice. So what was a Gakis doing changing beds?' Alexio bent and swept her up into his arms for the second time that day.

'I don't know.' Leaping nervous tension suddenly made Ione start talking a mile a minute and her heart was racing like an express train. 'I should've called the maids but I didn't. I knew you didn't realise who I was—'

Alexio lowered his arrogant dark head. She clashed with the midnight glitter of his beautiful eyes and her breath caught in her throat as he outlined the ripe curve of her lower lip with the teasing tip of his tongue. 'I realised when I saw your photograph and I was furious with you but very intrigued.'

He lowered her down onto the big bed in the bedroom next door. He reached out to remove one of her shoes, only to find himself clutching a shoe empty of a foot as Ione snaked at speed off the other side and backed awkwardly towards the bathroom.

'I'm sure you'll understand if I ask you not to lock the door, open any windows or seek a fire escape,' Alexio enumerated and he wasn't entirely joking. He watched the stones studding the entire heel of the shoe glitter with rainbow fire in the lamp light. 'Who gave you these?'

'Cosmas.' Her lovely face shadowed on that reference to her brother.

'Are they diamonds?' Alexio enquired.

His bride shrugged with all the innate unconcern of a Gakis born to wealth beyond avarice. 'Probably.'

'It's dangerous to flaunt that kind of wealth in public. It's also rather tacky,' Alexio delivered in exasperation.

Ione stiffened, kicked off the other shoe and went into the bathroom. 'You're a snob just like Papa said you were!' she slung.

As she vanished from view Alexio felt rather like a man

trying to imprison quicksilver between spread fingers. He dropped the offending shoe. 'Ione—?'

'Looking down on us because my grandparents weren't rich, important people. If I want to wear tacky shoes, I'll wear them!'

Ione may yet surprise you, Alexio reminded himself on the back of a suppressed groan.

With tears welling up in her eyes, Ione stared at her own reflection in the vanity mirror. If he regarded her adoptive family as vulgar people with tacky taste, how much more would he reel in horror from her true ancestry? A natural mother who had become pregnant with Ione and her twin during an extra-marital affair? A natural father who was a former politician brought down by his own corruption? A sister who carried on with rock stars and Sicilian tycoons? So was she now making a choice between finding that long-lost sister and staying married to Alexio?

'Ione…?'

Ione appeared back in the doorway. 'I shouldn't have shouted at you.'

Even bearing a close resemblance to a miniature ice queen, Alexio conceded with driven appreciation, his bride was incredibly beautiful.

'Do you want me to take my clothes off now?' Ione asked stonily, striving to act cool about the offer she was making.

Alexio parted his lips and then swallowed an appalling urge to laugh out loud. 'No, definitely not. I think it would be safer if we just go to bed and act like we've been married at least forty years and very rarely indulge in that sort of thing.'

Ione stared back at him in visible confusion and then reddened, uttered a strangled gasp and slammed back into the bathroom. Alexio heard the bolt ram across the door without surprise. He wished he had checked the window first. She was as skittish as a cat on hot bricks. Why was everything so complicated with her? Was it him? Or was it her? And how was he planning to lure her back out of the bathroom?

Torn apart by a sense of humiliated rejection and hurt, Ione ran a bath for want of anything better to do. Tears were running down her cheeks. Why had she listened to all that stupid soft soap about him having been attracted to her from the very first time he had seen her? Why hadn't she just asked him why he hadn't done something about that supposed attraction at the time? Men said stuff like that but didn't mean it. He had to think that she was as thick as a brick to swallow a story like that. Burning for her? The chilliest and most reserved burn she had ever seen! Why, he hadn't even spoken to her that night three months ago except to tell her that he would not sleep on satin sheets!

Self-evidently, it had been a massive mistake to try and assert herself sooner than be suspected of shrinking. Though whose fault was it that she was nervous? Her fault for plunging herself into a wedding night that she had never expected to play a part in? Or his for keeping on lifting her off her feet with that awesome strength as though she were some kind of little toy doll? And what right had he to assume that she wasn't a virgin? How dared he insult her like that? For make no mistake, that was a grave insult to the honour of her family! He might sleep around…she did not.

Somehow that last unfortunate reflection only increased Ione's turmoil. He was her husband and she just didn't know what to do with him, didn't know what was going on inside her own head either. Surely she couldn't be falling in love with a guy who had tried not to laugh when she'd offered to take her clothes off?

Wrapped in a giant bath towel, Ione slid the bolt back and slowly opened the door. The bedroom was empty. Instant panic filled her. Had Alexio got fed up and abandoned her in the hotel? Had he done to her what *she* had done to him? An awful chill gripped Ione and she fled across the room to look into the sitting room.

Having made several necessary calls, Alexio tossed the phone aside, straightened from his elegant lounging stance against the dining table and smiled at her. The relief that washed over Ione made her knees knock together. Steadying herself with one hand on the door handle, she went pink. 'I'll…I'll just go to bed, then,' she announced breathlessly.

'Good idea,' Alexio commented deadpan, suppressing his irreverent grin with all his might. For once, her lovely face had revealed her every thought. No, there was nothing dense about his bride and she might not look Greek but she thought like a Greek, all right. The very instant she'd found him absent, she had suspected revenge. She didn't trust him, not one inch. In fact he very much doubted that she had ever trusted any man and he frowned as he made that deduction.

Dropping the towel, Ione scrambled into the bed and lay between the cold sheets trying not to shiver. If practice made perfect, he was sure to be really good at it, she told herself. He was a great kisser. But there was a huge amount of other stuff that came between the kissing and the rest of it. She supposed she would have to pretend she liked it even if she didn't. She wondered what pretending would demand of her and whether or not he would be able to tell the difference. He was certainly taking his time about joining her.

Ione checked her watch. Ten minutes had passed. Not exactly enthusiastic, was he? Her soft mouth compressed. He just had no consideration. He might be gorgeous but he was an insensitive pig. She should have said no up front. Wedding night or not, she should have told him that it was absolutely medieval for him to expect her to sleep with him so soon! But then how many women had slept with him on the first date? She wished they had had the chance to date. He would still have been *waiting* at the end of six months!

Alexio strolled into the bedroom. He was feeling good about the decision he had just made. It had finally dawned on him that possibly a little restraint in the bedroom might pay dividends in the field of bridal trust and appreciation. His father had been quite right on one count. Alexio was not used to women who ran in the opposite direction. In fact the shock of that experience was still sinking in on him. That with her fear of heights she had also negotiated a two-storey fire escape stung.

As Ione's gaze settled on Alexio's lean, dark, devastating face a helpless little shiver of apprehensive heat travelled through her taut length. She met brilliant dark golden eyes and her heart hammered.

'I just came in to say goodnight,' Alexio imparted.

'S-sorry?' she stammered.

'I'll sleep in the other room. It's very late and you must be exhausted,' Alexio murmured smooth as glass.

Clutching the sheet to her chest, Ione stared at him with widening green eyes of total disconcertion. 'But...but this is our wedding night—'

Alexio shifted a fluid, expressive brown hand. 'We have the rest of our lives to spend together. Sharing a bed is only one small part of marriage...'

Only one *small* part? It was their wedding night and he

couldn't be bothered making love to her! The shock of such casual indifference from a male of his reputation hit Ione hard. Humiliated beyond belief, she fell back against the pillows and shut her eyes tight as she sucked in a tremulous breath. He didn't want her. He didn't even intend to occupy the same room.

'I'm prepared to wait,' Alexio completed huskily.

Even the vaguest notion of herself as being appealing now for ever buried, Ione sat up again in one driven motion. 'You can wait *for ever* as far as I'm concerned!' she gasped strickenly. 'I've never been so insulted in all my life!'

'Insulted? *How* have I insulted you?' Alexio demanded, the volume of his voice rising.

Ione was blinded by tears and her throat was closing over, but rage and hurt were eating her alive. 'First, you accuse me of dressing like a hooker. Then you accuse me of not being a virgin and finally...'

'Maybe you should have stayed off the fire escape,' Alexio slotted in lethally as she paused to gather in a sustaining breath.

'And *finally*,' Ione relaunched in sobbing condemnation, 'you tell me you don't even *want* me!''

'What sort of nonsense is that? Is this the reward I get for trying to be considerate and unselfish?' Alexio raked back at her, his volatile temper flaring on the strength of his annoyance at having what he had deemed to be a major compromise and sacrifice thrown back in his teeth. 'If I'd followed my own inclinations, I'd have busted down that bathroom door, hauled you out of that bath and flattened you to that bed an hour ago!'

Ione focused on him in sharp disconcertion.

Belatedly conscious that that had not been the most confidence-inducing confession he could have made, Alexio raked long brown fingers through his luxuriant black hair and breathed between gritted teeth. 'But that was only a fleeting fantasy born of frustration, naturally *not* an urge I would have acted on.'

Stilling, Ione processed that new information and her soft mouth fell open. Considerate? Unselfish? Those were not words or indeed abilities she had ever associated with men. Men always put themselves first. Even the brother she had adored, the brother who had been so kind to her, would never have made himself uncomfortable on her behalf. But when it dawned on her that Alexio was actually offering to sleep elsewhere because he had assumed that that was what *she* wanted even though it wasn't what *he* wanted, she was utterly transfixed by the concept. In that instant, he rose in her estimation one hundred per cent. In fact he soared so very high in her blitzed imagination that a pair of wings and a halo would not have been out of his reach.

Ione gave him a dizzy smile of appreciation that just grew and grew until her whole face glowed. 'Of course, I want you to stay…you're my husband,' she reminded him unevenly.

Entrapped by that glorious smile, Alexio stared back at her with shimmering golden eyes and then, without any perceptible thought preceding the action, he came down on his knees on the bed and reached for her in the same motion.

Each of them heading in the same direction, their mouths crashed up together and locked in a passionate onslaught. He framed her face with his hands, beautiful eyes hot with desire, snatched in a ragged breath and went back to her lush mouth for more. He captured her lips again and again, sensual, searching and so intense that her whole body trembled in the circle of his arms. Her hands curved to his well-shaped head and then her fingertips laced into his springy black hair to hold him to her.

It was as if there were a hungry fire inside her, licking up through every skincell. The plundering quest of his tongue only sent the flames shooting higher. A low moan was dredged from her as he tipped her back against the pillows with easy strength and crushed her beneath his superior weight. She arched her back helplessly, conscious only of the throbbing ache of her nipples and the shockingly strong need to push her sensitised breasts into abrasive contact with the fabric of his jacket.

'I'm wearing too many clothes,' Alexio husked, angling back from her to shrug free of his suit jacket, but losing concentration at the sight of her small, beautifully formed breasts crowned by delicate buds the colour of tea roses.

Only then realising that the sheet between them had slipped, Ione felt hot colour flood her cheekbones and she wrenched at the sheet instinctively, but it was pinned in place beneath a powerful male thigh.

'Don't...you're perfect,' Alexio breathed hoarsely, his sizzling gaze pinned to her breasts with flatteringly intense interest as he lowered his proud dark head to taste a straining pink peak.

As a tiny whimper parted her lips, the shimmering dart of almost painful arousal jackknifed through her and centred at the honeyed heart of her. Heartbeat hammering and breathless, she looked up at him, met his extraordinary eyes set beneath curling black lashes and felt the surge of wildfire reaction roar through her. Her whole body felt haywire, restive, hot with wanton craving. She did not have the will-power to shift so much as an inch from him, and the strength of her own response to him terrified her.

*   *   *

'I'll take my time, *agape mou*,' he swore in dark-timbred sensual promise, brushing his fingertips along the fragile curve of her jawbone. 'I'll make it good.'

In a lithe movement, Alexio sprang off the bed and began to undress. Dry-mouthed, Ione watched him unbutton his shirt, disclosing a muscular wedge of bronzed chest sprinkled with a riot of dark curls. Peeling off his well-cut trousers to strip down to a pair of dark boxer shorts, he discarded everything in a careless heap. Her fascination struggled with the return of her tension. From his wide shoulders to his long, powerful, hair-roughened thighs, he was all hard angles and lean muscle, potently male, breathtakingly spectacular. The boxer shorts travelled south. He angled a wicked grin over the dismayed eyes she shut just a second too late, surveyed the pink blossoming in her cheeks.

'Now you know for sure that I want you,' Alexio teased, the mattress giving beneath his weight as he shifted closer and let his breath fan her burning face before delving the tip of his tongue in a provocative slide between her parted lips.

'Yes.' Ione collided with his vibrant eyes and her head fell back on a long gasping sigh as he ran the palm of his hand over her straining nipples.

'You're so sensitive there, *yineka mou*.' With an appreciative groan, he cupped her swollen breasts, stroking the distended peaks with his fingers and extending the sweet torment with the hot, hungry provocation of his mouth.

Ione trembled and moaned out loud, twisting closer, pushing up to him and finally digging her hands into his hair to drag his lips back up to hers. Her head was swimming with the force of her own explosive response, every part of her slender, straining body on red alert. With every probe of his tongue, the taunting pulse of need between her thighs became more unbearable.

'Let me pleasure you,' Alexio said throatily, plotting a leisurely path down a quivering slender thigh through the pale soft curls to the moist, damp centre of her.

'Oh…' Without warning, even the smallest trace of control was wrenched from Ione by sensation. Her hips executed a feverish shift against the sheet, her hands clenching as the beat of her own hunger grew and she was powerless to prevent it. The wild excitement was building higher, tiny cries breaking on her lips as she squirmed, feverishly struggling to somehow satisfy the ache of her own tortured longing.

He shifted over her, hard, handsome features intent, golden eyes molten on her passion-glazed face. As he tipped up her thighs, he pressed a tender kiss on her swollen mouth and muttered hoarsely, 'I'll be gentle…I don't want to hurt you.'

The hot probe of him against her tender entrance was a sensual shock that made her still and then he entered her inch by incredible inch, all heat and pressure and alien maleness. She tensed in apprehension, astonished by the pleasurable feel of his invasion. At the momentary stab of pain she loosed a stifled moan and then he sank deep into her and she rose against him in startled response. The frantic excitement pounded through her again, electrifying, utterly controlling and she surrendered to the dark, deep, pulsing pleasure until he dragged her resistless to some crazy height where nothing but sensation ruled. Sharp, sweet ecstasy raked through her and expanded into an explosive cascade of delight and blew her into a thousand glittering pieces.

He shuddered over her in his own completion and a fierce burst of tenderness filled Ione and she closed her arms round him even more tightly, tears of wonderment sparkling in her softened eyes.

'That was extraordinary…' Alexio lifted his tousled dark head and looked down at her with dark-as-midnight eyes, noting the faint purple shadows that betrayed her exhaustion. His heart-stopping smile curving his wide sensual mouth as he rearranged them into a more relaxed huddle. Holding her slight body close, he dropped a kiss on her brow. 'Go to sleep now, *agape mou*. It's almost dawn.'

But he was the one who fell asleep and she lay watching him, in thrall to her own fascination and the quite unfamiliar sense of buoyant happiness consuming her. He slept in a careless sprawl with the sheet tangled round his hips and took up more than his fair share of the bed. She knew she was falling in love, knew there was not the slightest thing she could do about it. The freedom she had craved had been superseded by an infinitely more powerful craving to be with him.

All that was demanded from her was a leap of faith and the willingness to believe that Alexio would never treat her with the same callous lack of feeling that her father had demonstrated towards her mother…

CHAPTER SIX

ALEXIO watched Ione emerge from the changing room.

Radiant in an emerald-green shift dress that was a stunning foil for her bright eyes and wealth of platinum fair hair, Ione did a twirl. 'Well?'

Alexio was in search of a flaw but the dress wasn't too tight, wasn't too short and only her slim arms were bare. Even so, he still thought she looked too eye-catching. Paris was a very cosmopolitan city but heads turned wherever they went. Ione had the stylish cool and confidence that all true Parisians admired, but more than anything else she had that most basic and blatant of currencies: classic and sensational beauty of a calibre rarely seen.

'You've got to like this one,' Ione insisted with an impish smile. 'What's the matter with you?'

Alexio really didn't know. He had no idea why he always wanted to cover her up. He was not a possessive man. Crystal had worn outrageous clothes and, aside of his irritation over her constant hunger for attention, what his late fiancée had worn had never bothered him. But Ione only had to allow his chauffeur a glimpse of thigh as she alighted from the limo and he could feel his tension rising. She just didn't have a clue how beautiful she was. But sooner or later the supreme power that was hers would dawn on her and Alexio definitely didn't want that to happen when he was not around.

Ione's lush mouth pouted and she glided up to him. 'Are you bored?'

'No, I love a floorshow…I just prefer it in private,'

Alexio confided, his dark, deep drawl lowering to an intimate purr that sent a responsive shiver down her slender spine.

Drawn by the flare of gold in his smouldering gaze, Ione leant closer, starry eyes welded to his lean, dark, devastating features. Bare inches from him as she was, her senses delighted in his achingly familiar male scent. Three weeks of round-the-clock exposure to Alexio had barely touched the surface of her joy in him and certainly brought her no closer to satiation. She had been delighted when he'd sent her team of bodyguards back to Greece and replaced them with men who treated her with respect. In fact, the more time she spent with Alexio, the more she marvelled at the sheer rightness of their being together.

But throughout those same days and nights Ione's conscience had weighed ever more heavily on her. If Alexio ever found out the truth of *why* she had married him, how would he feel? If he learned that she had planned from the outset to walk out on their marriage, any trust he had in her and any respect or affection would be destroyed. No man deserved to be used by a woman merely as an escape from an unhappy home life. A chill of fear ran through her at the very thought of Alexio ever discovering how low she had once been prepared to sink.

Suppressing that anxiety, she made herself think instead about the wonderful honeymoon they had shared. Alexio had gone to public school in England but he had spent his university years at the Sorbonne. He spoke fluent French and he had shown her an insider's view of the city he loved. He had let her drag him round the Musee Marmottan to see Monet paintings and then had delighted her a week later with a surprise trip to Monet's house at Giverny. She had been enchanted by the pink villa with its green shutters and the glorious gardens and ponds created by the famous artist to serve as inspiration for his own paintings.

But the images that would remain longest with her were more intimate: getting soaked by the unpredictable water jets in the Parc Citroen and then thoroughly kissed even though she looked like a drowned rat; walking hand in hand along the Seine while Alexio explained that he had never been romantic and, in the midst of that macho proclamation, told her that when the breeze caught her hair she resembled a maiden from Arthurian legend; watching excited children sail toy boats in the Luxembourg gardens until Alexio pulled her into the circle of his arms and groaned, 'I don't know what you're doing to me but for the first time in my life I can honestly see myself wanting to have a baby with a woman.'

That particular recollection still filled Ione with a deep and happy sense of acceptance. And last but not least was the fabulous birthday cake which he had ordered for dinner the night before in honour of her twenty-third birthday. She fingered the Victorian ring that he had given her. It was a 'regard' ring, the first letter of each jewel spelling out that message, and she had been touched and pleased that he had taken the time to choose something so special as a gift.

Leaving the boutique on the Champs-Elysées, they went back to the townhouse to dine. Later they were attending the opera. As they went upstairs to dress after their meal Ione said ruefully, 'I'll be sad when we leave Paris—'

'We don't have to yet. Allow me thirty-six hours in London and I'll come back and base myself here for one more weekend—'

'You have business in London?' Ione looked up at him in surprise. 'Could I come with you?'

'You'd be bored out of your mind, *agape mou*.' Alexio

sighed. 'I'll be tied up in meetings all day and the company apartment I use over there isn't up to much.'

Brimming on her lips was the assurance that she wouldn't mind in the slightest, would indeed even consider camping out on a park bench if it meant she could stay near him. But common sense and pride mercifully intervened. After an entire three weeks of his attention, it was greedy of her to begrudge him a single night away from her. Nor was being possessive and demanding the way to impress him with her newfound maturity. Indeed, that sort of behaviour would only alienate him.

She loved Alexio with an intense passion that she had never dreamt she could feel and she was happier than she had known it possible to be. He might not love her, but he certainly did seem to care about her and he treated her better than she had ever been treated in her entire life. He was affectionate, humorous, charming and incredibly sexy at any hour of the day and sometimes she just couldn't believe that he was hers.

'Think of how rampant I'll be when I fly back,' Alexio growled in sensual threat, tugging her backwards into his arms on the threshold of their bedroom.

Ione grinned, snaking back into contact with his big, powerful frame. 'You're always rampant,' she teased, and she loved that reality for his passion made her feel like the most irresistible woman in the world.

'Stop doing that,' Alexio groaned as she arched her slim hips in sinuous, shameless encouragement into the hard, virile maleness of him.

Ione reddened, momentarily taken aback by her own behaviour, but the knowledge that they had only one more night before their idyllic honeymoon came to an effective end was a more potent inducement and she whispered unevenly, '*Make* me…'

'Not too long ago your idea of an invitation was looking longingly at me across a dining table. It was rather sweet but this is more exciting,' Alexio confided with hoarse appreciation as he spun her round and without hesitation captured her lush mouth with the hard, drugging force of his own.

The sheer hunger he made no attempt to hide exploded through her slender length like a depth charge that sent ripples of sensual shock through her every fibre. With a helpless little moan, she leant into him for support and he gathered her up, sent the door crashing shut with a powerful shoulder and tumbled her down on the bed.

'Day or night, I can't get enough of you...' Lean, strong face taut with all the passion of his volatile temperament, Alexio gazed down at her and, for the merest instant, his stunning golden eyes betrayed a mixture of surprise and faint discomfiture as he made that acknowledgement.

Gotcha, Ione reflected in an entirely different spirit of one-upmanship from that which she had once embraced in his vicinity. Her face stilled as she instinctively concealed the first revealing rush of her own happy satisfaction with that state of affairs. Any time of the day or night, he was welcome. Desire was only a beginning: she knew that, but without that desire any hope of his returning her love some day would have been doomed. For a male as passionate as Alexio, it would take more than a meeting of minds and goals to build a strong marriage.

'What are you thinking about?' Alexio demanded huskily as he stood over her, wrenching off his clothes with a flattering degree of impatience. 'You're wearing that little sneaky look you get when you're plotting something.'

'Sneaky?' Startled, Ione looked up at him in dismay. 'Plotting?'

His irrepressible wolfish grin slashed his bronzed features and made her heart clench on a fierce flood of love. 'I'm onto you *agape mou*. That tranquil lack of expression invariably means you're deep in intriguing thoughts.'

He was right and that shook her.

'I guess concealing your emotions comes naturally to you. That's how you operate around your father.'

Conscious of the more serious note in his dark drawl and the penetrating light in his keen scrutiny, Ione paled and turned her head away.

'Minos is an intimidating man. Strong men shake when he loses his temper,' Alexio remarked with a studied light-ness of tone. 'But you don't need to practice that kind of caution in my vicinity. I may lose my temper occasionally but I don't ever lose control of my fists.'

'That's good to know…but I really don't know why you're taking the trouble to tell me that.' With a slight tremor in her strained voice, Ione refused to be drawn, for it was not the first time in recent days that Alexio had raised a similar subject and she knew that she could not afford to trust him with any confidences of what her life had been like on Lexos. For to do so would put him at risk.

Didn't he know that curiosity had killed the cat? The habit of silence on the subject of her father's abuse was as engrained in her as it had been in her mother and her brother. But her father's violent outburst that night over dinner just over a month ago had left Alexio uneasy and, as time went on, she was aware that he had become more suspicious of exactly what he had witnessed and inter-rupted. She had the uncomfortable feeling that something in her own behaviour must have served to rouse those suspicions.

Frustration currented through Alexio as he saw her ex-quisite face shutter. The past was a closed book to Ione.

It was as if she had been born on the day of their wedding for she never mentioned her childhood or indeed any of her relatives, living or dead. And now her withdrawal was pronounced.

'Now, where were we?' Alexio teased, switching mental gears with ease and coming down on the bed beside her to angle her up against his bare, hair-roughened chest and run down the zip on her dress.

With sure hands he removed the garment and pushed her hair out of his path to let his expert mouth trace a provocative path across the exposed nape of her neck. She quivered, suddenly wild with hunger for him, and in an awkward movement she twisted round and pushed her mouth in a seeking, blind gesture into his. She felt safe, so safe with him, but she also knew that if she told him too much he would *not* be safe from her father's fury.

Alexio held her back from him for a moment. His eyes were the colour of rich honey as they sought her evasive gaze. 'What's wrong?'

'Nothing…' Even as he looked at her with those glorious eyes, the heat and the promise of his hard male arousal was already gaining mastery over her. Her breasts ached, their tender peaks swollen and stiff.

Spreading her slender thighs to either side of his, he undid her bra. Suddenly breathless, her heart pounding in her own eardrums, she let her head fall back and arched her spine so that her pouting, sensitive flesh grazed the dark thicket of black curls hazing his pectoral muscles.

'We're going to be late for the opera…' Alexio breathed with thickened purpose and, knotting one hand into her bright hair, he tilted her back with care until her taut spine met the mattress and then brought his urgent mouth down to tease at her straining nipples.

Fire leapt straight to the moist triangle between her

thighs. She jerked and gasped and then fell into the plundering kiss that followed like a drowning swimmer. Her fingers woven into his luxuriant hair, she surrendered to the dark pleasure of pure sensation as his expert hands roved over her quivering, sensitised body.

'You're an enchantress...' Alexio growled, staring down at her with smouldering intensity, his appreciative gaze absorbing her rapt expression. 'When you lose yourself in my arms, I have a hell of a job staying in control.'

'That's a complaint?' Ione whispered before he pressed his warm, carnal mouth to a pulse-point beneath her collarbone and his lean, sun-darkened hands proceeded to plot an erotic path down over her squirming, responsive length.

Within a very little while, she was even more inflamed with longing and whimpering beneath his electrifying caresses, her entire being in thrall to his. No longer could she resist the urge to touch him in turn, and her exploring fingers followed the narrow furrow of dark hair that bisected his taut, lean stomach and almost reached the hot, hard tautness of his throbbing shaft before he clamped a restraining hand over hers with a rueful groan.

'I can't wait.' In a purposeful movement, Alexio rearranged her. Anchoring himself between her parted thighs, he entered her with a slow, delicious strength that made her moan out loud with pleasure.

And then there was nothing but him and the way he could make her feel driven, possessed and yet weak with love. She felt him tremble with the force of his own fierce need and she curved round him in abandonment, scanning the raw tension of passion etched in his darkly handsome face. He urged her to explosive fulfilment with powerful thrusts and the stormy excitement overwhelmed her in a breathtaking surge of ecstasy that wrung her out in the aftermath.

'We'll be very, very late, *agape mou*,' Alexio husked, dropping a kiss on her slight shoulder and licking the salt from her skin with an earthy enjoyment that made her melt. 'Do you mind?'

'Mind?' She minded nothing that he did while he held her close and looked down at her with those wonderful dark eyes that made her heart leap. 'No.'

'It's amazing how well we match,' Alexio informed her with indolent male satisfaction and she almost smiled at his innocence.

For even in the space of three weeks, Ione had been careful to pick up on his preferences and adjust herself accordingly. She had been mortified when it had finally dawned on her that she had rather juvenile tastes in fashion. She supposed that in some ways that was understandable, for she had never got to go through the natural phase of defining her own identity by what she'd worn in adolescence.

Somehow, without ever actually saying so, Alexio had managed to let her know that the type of outfit she had worn to the airport was most popular with teenage girls. And, at almost twenty-three, she ought to have been beyond that stage. Quite how his attitude meshed with the often spectacular fashion statements flaunted by his late fiancée, Crystal, Ione had no very clear idea. But one reality she did accept: Alexio had loved Crystal and love could be blind. As she had no such bank of reassuring love to depend on, it had seemed to her that she had no choice but to put his approval above her own inclinations.

So, her beloved shoes with their diamond heels that seemed to strike Alexio as the ultimate in vulgarity had remained in her wardrobe. Then there was the fact he liked to get up very early in the morning, not to mention his decided preference for Greek food when she would have happily sampled international cuisine at every meal. It was all a case of been there, done that for him, she reflected with loving forgiveness.

'I'm not fond of opera,' Alexio confided lazily.

Ione suppressed a sigh.

Alexio leant over her, brilliant eyes mocking. 'But I know you've been looking forward to it all week, so we will go.'

'Then we'd better hurry!' Galvanised into action, Ione peeled off her watch to toss it on the cabinet by the bed and snaked free of him to flee into the bathroom to have the fastest shower on record.

Thirty minutes later, her hair swept up to hold the magnificent amethyst and diamond tiara that matched her necklace and earrings, and clad in a figure-hugging lilac sheath that split just above the knee to reveal a glimpse of slender leg, Ione looked in vain for the watch she had carelessly discarded. It was in neither the tumbled bedding nor on the carpet, and then she recalled that the top drawer of the cabinet had been lying open before she'd gone for her shower and she tugged it wide again. Smiling as she reclaimed her watch from the drawer, she saw a photograph.

Sliding the watch back on her wrist, she nudged aside the condom packet, for it was Alexio's cabinet, and reached for the photo of the smiling bikini-clad brunette. Her heart hammering chokily in what felt like her throat, she slowly sank down on the side of the bed to study Crystal Denby. Alexio's socialite fiancée had been extremely attractive and even Ione's critical eye recognised the appeal of her voluptuous figure and long, perfect legs, not to mention the provocative sparkle of her dark eyes and sexy smile. Alexio had taken that photograph. She knew it in her bones. Crystal had been posing for her lover, confident of his admiration.

Her tummy queasy and her skin chilling over, Ione replaced the photo where she had found it and shut the drawer again. But she was trembling and she felt as if Alexio had stuck a knife into her without warning. Why did he keep a picture of Crystal within easy reach of their marital bed? How often did he look at it? Well, obviously it was there to be looked at, *grieved* over…

She felt hollow inside and simultaneously sick with rage and pain. Throughout their honeymoon, she had been determined not to think of Crystal. She had been equally careful not to ruin her own contentment with the reflection that Alexio had probably shared many of the same outings and much of the same passion with the lovely brunette. Such wounding thoughts would have been pointless, but the discovery of that photograph had blown her liberal and sensible approach to their marriage right out of the water.

Alexio emerged from the dressing room. She stole a single glance at his lean, dark, devastating features, imprinting him on her mind's eye with agonised hurt and resentment foaming up inside her. She had ditched her pride for him, even taken a rain check on her longing to be reunited with her twin sister for him, and she had exerted herself in every way to be the wife that *he* wanted. And wasn't that where she had gone wrong in the weakness of loving him to distraction? What about what *she* wanted?

'Turn round,' Alexio murmured in his dark, deep, throaty drawl. 'You look amazing in that dress.'

Slender spine taut, Ione spun round from the window, eyes glittering bright as emeralds in her triangular face. 'I saw the photo of Crystal Denby you have in the drawer by the bed!'

A very slight frownline drew his winged ebony brows together and his stunning golden eyes narrowed in a questioning look. 'And?' Alexio prompted, refusing to react having always been his first line of defence in potential scenes with her sex.

That single word sent Ione rocketing from hurt to blinding, ungovernable rage. *And?* As if it should mean nothing to her that her husband cherished another woman's picture, as if she had no right whatsoever to comment on the fact, as if only a very unreasonable woman would dare to object. Ione read meanings into that single word that he could never have dreamt.

'If you don't get rid of that photo, I'm leaving you!' Ione heard herself fling back, and her own shock at the melodramatic threat that emerged of its own seeming accord from her lips was greater than his.

Alexio regarded her with sardonic disbelief writ large in his lean, strong face. His wide shoulders were squared, long, powerful legs braced slightly apart. 'If we don't leave now for the opera, it won't be worth our while going.'

Momentarily silenced by that complete sidestepping of the entire issue, Ione stared at him in a tempestuous fury. 'You think I want to go and watch a stupid opera when you've got a picture of another woman in our bedroom?'

'Don't shout at me,' Alexio countered very soft and low, stormy golden eyes resting on her with a silent intimidation she could feel.

Ione's stomach flipped over, the same sick sensation of fear that came over her in her father's presence attacking her for the very first time in Alexio's. But the same defiance that had brought her into regular conflict with Minos Gakis while her mother had still been alive leapt up even stronger. 'You have insulted me,' she framed with fierce conviction.

Alexio was cursing the inefficiency of the domestic staff, who had been instructed to make a clean sweep of all such memorabilia, for he had made little use of the townhouse over the past two years. But then, only a wife would rifle through his personal effects, Alexio reflected with all the annoyance of a male who hated complications.

'In what way have I insulted you?' he murmured, and that precise tone of boredom had in the past proved more than sufficient to deflate most women.

That laconic intonation had the same effect on Ione as hot coals shovelled onto a dying fire.

'I'm your wife. She was a tramp!'

The instant that inflammatory word left her lips, Ione was ashamed of herself. So disrespectful and cruel a reference to a woman who had been dear to him was decidedly beyond the bounds of what was forgivable.

Alexio froze in receipt of that allegation. Outrage flashing into his stormy golden gaze, he surveyed her with a distaste that was more than sufficient punishment for her reckless tongue. 'I respect her memory and so must you for I will not tolerate your jealousy,' he said harshly.

'I'm not jealous of her...' Ione whispered hoarsely, her aching throat closing over on that anguished denial.

But Alexio said nothing. He simply strode out of the room. Disconcerted, Ione closed her eyes in despair over her own foolishness. A minute later, she hurried after him, but by the time she reached the top of the stairs the front door below was thudding shut on his departure.

Jealous, *yes*, Ione then conceded painfully. She *was* bitterly jealous of the woman who had once held Alexio's heart. It didn't matter that Crystal was dead: her memory lived on. He never mentioned her, but then she had not

asked any questions for, the more important Alexio became to her, the less she had been able to bear any thought
of his late fiancée. But why shouldn't he keep a photograph of Crystal? It had not even been on open display.
Now because she had not had the wit or the self-discipline
to mind her own business, she had ruined the last night of
their honeymoon.

Hopeful that he would return and determined to make
a sincere apology, Ione went down to the drawing room
to wait. She was all shaken up and really scared of the
damage she had done to their relationship. Why was it,
though, that she was always doomed to be second-best in
the eyes of those she cared about?

The same hurting thread seemed to stretch through her
whole life. Cosmas had been the child most dear to his
parents' hearts, Ione merely the baby in need of a home
who had roused Amanda's loving and generous compassion. And here she was, second-best to her husband as
well, for Alexio would never have married her had Crystal
still been alive. Yet in spite of that knowledge she had
still contrived to fall head over heels in love with him and
hold back from what had once been her most driving ambition: her desperate longing to be reunited with her twin
sister.

Of course, she did eventually intend to defy her father
and tell Alexio the truth about her background in the hope
that he would understand how much finding her sister,
Misty, meant to her. So why hadn't she done it yet? Why
hadn't she told him? And the answer came back loud and
clear and made her ashamed of her own cowardice. She
had stalled on telling Alexio that she was adopted because
she was afraid that if he knew he would think less of her
for not being a true Gakis. After all even Cosmas, who

had loved her, had heartily pitied her for not being *born* into the family.

But now she had to live with the knowledge that Alexio had walked out on her in total disgust at her unpleasantness, which was much, much worse, Ione reflected wretchedly.

When Alexio entered the drawing room some hours later, his lean, strong, face taut, he found Ione clad in very fetching silk nightwear and curled up on a sofa fast asleep.

Ione woke up only when Alexio scooped her up into his arms. Looking up at his bronzed, dark features and the faint smile curving his wide, sensual mouth, she blinked in confusion and her heart crashed against her ribcage, but she still spoke the last thought that had occurred to her before she'd drifted off into slumber. 'How would you like it if I kept a photo of Yannis in our bedroom?'

Alexio stopped dead in his tracks, complete disconcertion powering through him in receipt of that sudden question. 'I wouldn't have it,' he growled without a second of hesitation, and silence stretched before comprehension stepped in and dark colour scored his hard cheekbones.

Mollified by that admission, Ione screened her gaze and muttered ruefully, 'I shouldn't have said what I did.'

Infuriated by that crack about Yannis and recognising that he had been stitched up, Alexio shrugged and began to undress. Nothing short of thumbscrews would have persuaded him to mention the fresh opera booking he had made for the weekend.

Aware that she had ducked the genuine apology she had intended to make, Ione breathed guiltily, 'Alexio, I—'

'I have a six o'clock flight to make in a few hours' time,' he incised in cool interruption. 'Let's shelve any serious conversations until I get back.'

Realising in dismay that the topic of Crystal now appeared to be a total no-go area, Ione slid out of her wrap, got into bed and breathed in deep. 'But I have something I want to tell you and if I wait, I might lose my nerve.'

A frown pleating his ebony brows, Alexio focused on her with smouldering dark golden eyes.

'It's a family secret and Papa warned me not to tell you because he doesn't like it to be known,' Ione rattled off in a rush. 'But I wasn't born into the Gakis family...I was *adopted* into it.'

Alexio regarded her with unconcealed disbelief. 'Have you been drinking?'

Ione scrambled back out of bed, disappeared into the dressing room and emerged again in a breathless surge. 'That's my sister, my twin...' Ione extended the tiny baby snap she had dug out of her attaché case. 'Her name's Misty.'

Alexio took the little black and white baby photo between thumb and forefinger and stared back at Ione with a stunned light in his gaze. 'You are serious about this?'

He both looked and sounded so shocked that Ione paled and dived back into bed. 'A nurse took a picture of her before we were parted.'

'Adopted...' Alexio sank down on the edge of the divan, frowning golden eyes lodged to her. '*When* were you adopted?'

'I was only a few weeks old.' Ione went on to explain that she had not been as healthy as her twin at birth and her natural mother had decided that she could not cope with a second baby who would require extra care and further medical treatment.

'What was the matter with you?' Alexio demanded.

'I was underweight and I had feeding problems...and the birth also left me with dislocated hips,' Ione said with a grimace. 'Papa wanted Mama to adopt a boy but she wanted me. He hoped that adopting me would somehow miraculously help Mama to conceive another son.'

'I have heard of that happen.' Alexio's keen gaze was intent on her strained profile, his intelligence warning him that he had strayed into a verbal minefield in which he had not the smallest experience. 'When did you find out that you were adopted?'

'I was so young, I can't even remember.'

'Where were you born?'

'London.'

Alexio could not conceal his astonishment. 'You were adopted from England?'

'I don't have a drop of Greek blood in my veins,' Ione admitted, sudden piercing regret assailing her when it was far too late to think better of what she had confided. He was appalled. It was written all over him. And she had not even got as far as admitting to her less than presentable birth ancestry, not to mention the unfortunate plight of a sister who was the mistress of some tycoon.

'To be Greek by adoption is the next best thing,' Alexio asserted in haste, his lean, sun-darkened hand closing over her clenched fingers in sincere sympathy. To comment that missing out on the Gakis gene pool might well be no great cause for sorrow would not be tactful. He was still in shock.

Ione didn't want his pity and an all-too-familiar sense of wounding rejection was gripping her. She cared, she cared far too much about what Alexio now thought of her. But why? What difference did it really make? She was *still* the Gakis heiress, *still* his wife and he *still* kept a picture of Crystal Denby in their bedroom. Yanking her hand free of his, she turned her back on him and closed her stinging eyes tight.

'I just thought you had the right to know,' she said flatly. 'But I don't want to talk about it any more. Goodnight.'

When Ione wakened the following morning, she was miserable when she realised that she had slept through Alexio's departure. But an enormous basket of beautiful flowers was brought to her an hour later. She opened the accompanying card.

'You are a Christoulakis now,' Alexio had written in the evident belief that it would be a comfort for her to know that no higher honour could be conferred upon a woman, and her eyes swam with tears even as she laughed.

Had she misunderstood him the night before? Foisted her own insecurities onto him? He had been very taken aback by the news that she had been adopted, but surely he could not have written that message had he been seriously concerned by what she had told him? She longed to be with him again and was furious with herself for giving way to her own emotional turmoil and freezing him out in the aftermath of their first row. Now she had thirty-six hours to wait until he flew home again. Why did she never have any sense when it came to Alexio?

She could always fly over to London and surprise him! The instant that idea occurred to Ione, it possessed her. The staff would know the address of his city apartment and when he finished his working day, she would be there waiting...

CHAPTER SEVEN

IONE was in an exuberant mood by the time the limousine her bodyguards had acquired for her pulled up in front of the apartment block late afternoon.

She was in London for the first time since her birth. Thanks to her adoptive mother, she was bilingual, but she had feared that the English that Amanda Gakis had always used with her children when she'd been alone with them might have grown a little rusty since her brother's death. However, she had tested herself out on the businessman seated next to her on the flight from Paris. He had been extremely chatty and had boosted her confidence by telling her that she spoke his language with only a slight and very charming accent.

Ione emerged from the lift and walked to the door of the apartment. Thinking better of using the spare key she had been delighted to find available in the townhouse, she rang the bell first just in case there were staff or indeed someone else staying there. She was on the brink of employing the key when the door swung wide.

A tall brunette with a mane of hair the colour of glossy chestnuts, her shapely figure enhanced by a smart black suit, looked out with a brimming smile that fell away in slow motion when she saw Ione.

Surprised, but assuming that the woman worked for Alexio in some capacity, Ione walked on into the hall. 'I'm Ione Christoulakis.'

'Pascale Fortier.' The svelte Frenchwoman let the door snap shut again on its own.

'Do you work for my husband?' Ione asked, strolling ahead into the main reception room and surveying it with some disappointment for it was so bland it might have been a hotel room. But then he had said it was a company flat and the presence of a third party made the possibility of a romantic dinner for two unlikely, Ione conceded in seething disappointment. Registering that that unexpected guest was taking a long time to respond to her question, Ione turned her head in enquiry.

'No...I don't work for Alexio.' Pascale was staring at her, coins of colour marking her exotic cheekbones, her attractive face hard. 'Was Alexio expecting you?'

'No.' Wondering why the brunette was emanating angry defensiveness, Ione tensed up as well. 'I gather you're staying here?'

The other woman shrugged a designer-clad shoulder and then gave her a malicious little smile. '*Tiens.* I suppose a wife must take precedence over a lover and I shall have to pack.'

Ione heard nothing beyond the first part of that declaration. Her skin turned clammy, shock reeling through her in an explosive wave. A *lover*? There was a rushing sound in her eardrums and the other woman's voice seemed to be coming from very far away. Then, in the space of a sickening instant that made her tummy lurch, everything fell into place: Alexio's smooth assurance that the London apartment wouldn't suit her and that he would be too busy to spend time with her. How foolish and blind she had been to the obvious!

Alexio had not wanted her to accompany him to London. He had had other plans for this thirty-six-hour break away from her. Ione felt as if the walls were closing in around her and the floor were breaking up beneath her feet. Heart clenching, she made herself look at Pascale with much keener attention. Another tall, beautiful and confident brunette in the style of Crystal Denby and very much the kind of woman that seemed to define Alexio's taste in her sex. So, how had she ever believed for one moment that a wife who was a small, slight blonde could have any enduring appeal for such a male?

Without another word, for pride alone was holding her together, Ione walked back out of the apartment. A tiny bead of perspiration trickled down between her breasts. Shattered by that encounter with Alexio's mistress, she was shaking. Yet it was also as if her brain had been cut in two. While on one level she was possessed with a blind, helpless craving to find some *other* explanation for the Frenchwoman's presence in Alexio's apartment, on another level she was already accepting that Alexio had planned to spend the night there betraying her in the arms of another woman. After all, hadn't even her own father warned her that Alexio would be unfaithful?

Her bodyguards awaited her in the ground floor reception and escorted her back to the underground car park. She knew exactly what her family would expect her to do in such circumstances: fly back to Paris, behave as though she had never come to London and indeed act as though nothing had happened. She had been raised to the tune of such double standards, taught that, while a woman must always maintain a decent reputation, a man might do as he liked as long as he was discreet. Her own mother had ignored her husband's infidelity to the best of her ability. But no such martyred soul eager to break out existed inside Ione.

Devastated as she was, she was already getting angry. When had she chosen to forget that their marriage was more of a business alliance than a personal relationship? When had she stopped thinking about Alexio's bad reputation for loving and leaving women? Love had blinded her. Love had filled her with unrealistic expectations and left her sick with humiliation and anguish. It was time to acknowledge her mistakes, call a halt to her own weakness and let Alexio know in no uncertain terms that she had no intention of tolerating his infidelity. Snatching up the phone, she ordered the chauffeur to take her to Alexio's office.

'No, don't announce me,' Ione told the wide-eyed receptionist who rose to greet her on the executive floor of the elegant building that housed Christoulakis Enterprises. 'I want to surprise my husband. Where is his office?'

Impervious to the obsequious secretary, who fell into step by her side and talked in anxious apology about some *terribly* important meeting due to begin in five minutes' time, Ione thrust open the door. Walking in rigid-backed, she leant back against the door to close it again.

Alexio was talking on the phone. Sunlight cascaded through the tall window behind him to pick up the sheen of his luxuriant black hair, the stunning angles and hollows of his superb bone structure, and then fire his extraordinary eyes to mesmeric pure gold as he looked up with a frown to see who had entered his office without permission.

Springing upright in one lithe, powerful motion, he exclaimed in surprise, *'Ione?'*

At first sight of Alexio, the cautious vein of protective detachment that Ione had thrown up between her brain and her emotions evaporated. Her heartbeat lodged in the foot of her tight throat and hammered there, making it difficult for her to breathe. His breathtaking smile flashed across his sensual mouth, lighting his lean, bronzed features with the mesmeric charisma that was so much a part of his raw, masculine appeal. That smile disconcerted her, for any onlooker might easily have been convinced that Alexio was delighted by the sudden arrival of his wife in London. But then didn't his ability to conceal his true reactions simply emphasise how truly low and sneaky and cunning he was?

Deep, dark anger stirred higher in Ione. Her already taut spine notched up another inch in rigidity and her chin lifted. Yet even while she hated him, she knew that she still loved and wanted him. 'I have only come here to tell you that our marriage is over.'

Smile ditching fast, Alexio lodged level dark golden eyes on her in apparent bewilderment. 'I beg your pardon?'

'Our lawyers will deal with the legalities of our separation,' Ione stated and snatched in a stark breath. 'I do not want to see you again, nor will I discuss my decision.'

'Believe me, *agape mou*…you are going to discuss this until dawn breaks tomorrow,' Alexio countered soft and low, brilliant eyes shimmering with a blaze of incredulous anger. 'I don't care what notion you have got into your head, you are *not* walking out on our marriage!'

Ione's facial muscles were so tight, she felt as though she were talking through a mask and the lips she parted were bloodless. 'I met your mistress at your apartment.'

Computing that new fact into the situation, Alexio's big, powerful frame tautened and his eyes darkened, his strong bone structure setting hard. 'I don't have a mistress. Pascale is an ex of mine, nothing more. She still has a key to the apartment and she contacted me when she arrived in London this morning. I told her that she could stay the night there but I said no to the dinner invite.'

A jagged laugh was wrenched from Ione as she remembered Pascale's face falling when she'd realised that it was Ione and not Alexio on the doorstep. 'What sort of a fool to you think I am?' she prompted tightly, fighting the high note of stress she could hear in her own voice.

'You're my wife and I expect you to *trust* me,' Alexio grated on a sudden fierce note of fury. 'I told my secretary to book me into a hotel for the night.'

'Of course, you wouldn't admit the truth unless I actually caught you in the *act* of betraying me,' Ione countered in bitter reproach, infuriated by what she deemed to be smooth and clever lies intended to make her doubt her own judgement. 'But I've seen enough to convince me that you're still the womaniser you always were. I won't live with an unfaithful husband—'

'Have you listened to one thing I've said?' Alexio launched back at her with savage bite, his golden gaze shimmering, his strong jawline set at an aggressive slant. 'No, you haven't. You judged me guilty before you even entered my office. You're not even giving me the chance to defend myself!'

'I know your reputation with women.' Ione flung her pounding head so high, her neck ached, her hard-won composure beginning to unravel at the seams. 'I won't accept such a marriage. I won't live with lies and pretences—'

'*Theos mou*…you're not going anywhere until this is sorted out!' Alexio thundered as he strode towards her, his outrage unconcealed.

'Thumping me or threatening me won't work either!' Ione gasped, backing away a step in spite of her attempt to make herself stand her ground.

'Thumping you?' Alexio froze as though she had exploded that same ground from beneath his feet. Pale beneath his bronzed skin, he surveyed her with shattered intensity, his brilliant eyes locking to the taut white triangle of her half-fearful, half-defiant face. 'You think that I would hit you?'

A shiver ran through Ione as she realised what she had betrayed in her distress.

'Your father *did* hit you…' Alexio framed a split second later, shock roaring through him in spite of the suspicions he had had. 'Do you think all men are like that? I've never struck a woman in my life, nor would I! How could you think I would harm you?'

Ione was trembling, her teeth chattering together. He had backed off from her as though she had attacked him. He was appalled by what he had learnt but there was a look of blunt masculine reproach in his level gaze that she could have believed him capable of meting out similar abuse. In shamed perplexity, she spun away for she had always felt safe with Alexio, had somehow known right from the beginning that in that way he was not at all like her father.

'For your own protection,' she breathed unevenly, 'you mustn't ever let Papa know that you know. He has ruined men for less.'

Alexio said nothing. Instead, he simply closed his arms round her from behind, magnifying the enormous confusion she was struggling to overcome. It was a warm, reassuring embrace, calculated not to either threaten or invade her space too much. What shook her was her own rampant desire to lean back into him, flip round and feel the hard strength and heat of his lean, muscular body against her just one more time. Just *one* more time before she walked away.

'He will never get to lay a finger on you again, *agape mou*,' Alexio swore hoarsely. 'I swear that. You will never return to Lexos. You will never be alone with him again. As long as he lives, you will be safe.'

Her eyes filled with anguished tears for she knew he meant every word of those assurances. And every skincell in her body was jumping, every pulse on red alert to make proper physical contact with the man she still loved. Making herself step away from Alexio in that instant was the hardest challenge she had ever faced. But he was bad for her, she reminded herself painfully. He might not be *all* bad but she could not live with a faithless man she could not trust. He had already hurt her and it was her duty to protect herself. If she stayed in their marriage, he would destroy her as surely as Minos Gakis had destroyed her adoptive mother.

'I need more,' Ione breathed shakily and, straining every sinew to overcome her own weakness, she moved out of the protective circle of his arms and turned round to face him again. 'More than you can give me.'

Alexio rested raw dark golden eyes on her. 'I haven't been unfaithful to you…and I will not be in the future either.'

Possibly he fully believed that, Ione thought wretchedly. Perhaps because she had caught him out before he could even succumb to the provocative Pascale's charms, guilt was making him credit that he could change. But it was too late. The writing was on the wall and she was painfully aware that there would be countless occasions when temptation came Alexio's way. He was an extraordinarily good-looking man and that reality combined with ruthless power and enormous wealth would encourage all too many women to see him as a challenge.

'It was a nice honeymoon,' Ione whispered with ragged sincerity. 'But I mean it as no offence when I say that I can do better than stay married to a man like you. A man who buried his supposed heart in another woman's grave—'

'*Ione*—' Alexio ground out in raw interruption.

'I want a man who loves me for myself and I would

sooner be alone than accept anything less. All my life, I've accepted less, but I won't do it any longer,' she swore in an agonised undertone. 'I deserve a life of my own and I intend to find my sister, Misty, and get to know her.'

'I will help you to find your sister but I won't help you to make a life *away* from me!' Lean, powerful face taut with strain, Alexio reached for her clenched hands and engulfed them in his. 'This is crazy. I don't think you've absorbed a single word I've said and you're very upset.'

Ione swallowed back the awful thickness in her throat. Leaving Alexio felt like trying to sacrifice one of her own limbs. As she dragged her hands from his the door opened without warning and Alexio expelled his breath in a driven hiss of frustration. Then silence fell. A bulky older man wearing an Arab headdress with his suit stood on the threshold with an expectant air of impatience.

'Your Excellency…' Switching into business mode, Alexio strode forward to greet him.

After exchanging several phrases in what Ione assumed to be Arabic, Alexio swung back to draw her forward and introduce her as his wife. The older man was an emir, whose lengthy foreign name went right over Ione's buzzing head. She forced a polite smile to her stiff lips, conscious that he had to be the VIP whose arrival Alexio's secretary had tried to warn her was imminent.

As the emir's party entered in his wake, Alexio tugged open the door into an adjoining office and, recognising that neither of them had any choice but to accept the interruption with good grace, Ione walked on through. 'Twenty minutes…please wait,' Alexio urged in a charged undertone, searching her evasive green eyes for agreement.

As he hesitated, visibly unwilling to leave her without that assurance, Ione nodded. The tension easing in his darkly handsome features, he closed the door again, leaving her alone. Ione drew in a sustaining breath and walked straight out through the other door into the corridor outside Alexio's office. It was easier this way, she told herself as she entered the lift, closely followed by her protection team. No more unpleasant arguments, no dragged-out, emotionally draining scenes at which she might risk losing impetus and conviction. She was weak where Alexio was concerned but she had meant every word she'd said to him. He could have all the Pascales he wanted now and continue to cherish his photos of Crystal, but she would have a life of her own too.

She told one of her bodyguards to call her a taxi and remove her suitcase from the limousine. When the taxi arrived, she informed the men whom Alexio had hired to dog her every footstep that she did not wish to be accompanied or followed. She asked the driver to take her to the station from which she could most easily catch a train to Norfolk.

She was taking the first necessary step towards finding her sister and it was a journey that she had dreamt of making many times in the past. Yet now, when she had finally claimed the right and the freedom to make that journey, she was choked by tears and literally torn apart by the knowledge that it was unlikely that she would ever see Alexio again. The actual prospect of living without him hit her then like a giant rock dropped from a height…and telling herself that she had been strong and had made the right decision was not of the smallest comfort.

It was after nine that evening when Ione got off the train and wearily waited for yet another taxi to pick her up from the rural station.

But she was finally within only a few miles of the house

where her sister had been living when she had written to Ione almost five years earlier. The taxi driver told her that Fossetts was a local landmark: a tall, narrow building with a steep roof and attic windows that from a distance lent it the quaint charm of a doll's house. As she thought about that letter, which her father had not allowed her to reply to or retain, Ione's throat ached. Would her sister be able to forgive her for that lack of response? And what were the chances of there *still* being someone living at Fossetts who either knew or remembered Misty?

Asking the driver to wait as she planned to spend the night at a local hotel, Ione approached the front door. She was very nervous. A well-built middle-aged woman answered the bell.

'I'm sorry to disturb you at this hour but I'm trying to trace a woman called Misty Carlton,' Ione explained tautly. 'She lived here about five years ago.'

The woman looked bemused. 'But not now, I'm afraid. Misty got married last year.'

'Married?' Ione echoed in considerable surprise.

'Why, yes…to Leone Andracchi. He's a very successful businessman and they have a little boy called Connor now. Misty's foster mother, Birdie Peace, still lives here but unfortunately she's out this evening.'

Shock and excitement made Ione's heart beat very fast. 'Could you give me Misty's address?'

Her momentarily chatty informant seemed discomfited by that more bold request. 'Well, I'm not sure I'm at liberty to do that. May I ask why you're trying to get in touch with Misty?'

Ione drew in a charged breath. 'I think…I mean, I *know* that she's my twin sister. I was adopted but she went into foster care. I've wanted to find my sister for a long time.'

For several tense seconds silence stretched while the

woman stared at Ione in frank disconcertion. 'My goodness, will you come inside and wait for Birdie to come
home?'

'Thank you, but I've been travelling all day and I'm
very tired.' Ione was reluctant to have to deal with the
brimming curiosity now visible in the older woman's face.
'Perhaps you could give me Misty's phone number…'

Minutes later, Ione got back into the taxi on knees that
felt as weak as cotton wool. She had it, she *had* the phone
number! She had also learnt that her sister was a couple
of hundred miles away in Scotland where she and her husband had a second home, but nothing could dim her joy
at finally having a concrete link to the twin from whom
she had been parted soon after birth. At that moment, be-
lieving that she might actually lift a phone and hear her
long-lost sister's voice on the line was almost too much
for Ione to credit.

Furthermore, it seemed that her father had lied about
her sibling's lifestyle, for the adventurous sister whom
Ione had naively believed would need her support and advice was already both happily married and a mother. She
was embarrassed by her own clear misconceptions about
her twin and grateful that she had had no opportunity to
reveal them and cause offence. Yet that discovery was also
another humbling moment of truth for Ione, who could not
help comparing her sister's apparent security with the humiliating reality that her own marriage had barely lasted
the length of the honeymoon.

Checking into the Belstone House hotel, Ione requested
a suite. In the seclusion of the gracious sitting room, her
first act was to order a meal for she was feeling dizzy from
lack of food. Then she studied the phone again and the
piece of paper bearing that all-important number. Common
sense told her that late at night was hardly a sociable hour

at which to call in the hope of speaking to her sister for the first time.

Baulked from the one act that might hopefully have banished Alexio to the back of her mind, Ione strove not to think instead about what her estranged husband might be doing at that exact moment. Hadn't she given him his freedom back? So why should he not take advantage of it? Alexio might well have enjoyed the romantic evening with Pascale that, at the outset of the day, Ione herself had hoped to share with him. After all, what would he have left to lose?

And that had been *her* choice. She trembled, tummy churning at the awful turmoil threatening to eat her alive. In a determined movement, she stripped all the rings he had given her from her hand and set them on the coffee-table. Walking through to the bedroom, she decided to have a quick shower and change into something more comfortable before her meal arrived.

But just suppose, another little voice piped up while she was in the shower, just suppose the explanation Alexio had given her about Pascale had been the truth? A pushy ex-girlfriend showing up without warning and making herself at home in the apartment with a view to persuading him into continuing their relationship in spite of his recent marriage? Ione groaned in shame at her own revealing train of thought. To even think in such a manner was to risk becoming the kind of wife who buried her head in the sand and swallowed any excuse, no matter how improbable it was.

Surely she would fall out of love again with Alexio? Surely her awareness of his true character would kill that love stone dead? But why was life so cruel? Why, when Yannis had been so fine a man, had she only been able to admire and respect him? And yet when Alexio had come along, she had seen all his flaws yet *still* she had let him steal her heart!

As she tied the sash on her light silk robe the noisy clackety-clack approach of a low-flying helicopter made Ione wince. She moved over to the window. Her heart skipped a beat in sheer shock when she saw a craft emblazoned in the unmistakable colours of Christoulakis Enterprises skimming in low over the hotel's illuminated topiary gardens and coming in to land out of view...

CHAPTER EIGHT

AS ALEXIO sprang from the helicopter he was still light-headed with the rage that had roared through him unabated all evening.

When he had walked into that office next to his own and found it empty, he had been shattered by what felt like the ultimate stab in the back. That Ione should have agreed to wait and had then broken her word had been, on his terms, an unconscionable act of betrayal. Prior to that, he had been ready to make allowances for the fact that she was the daughter of a man who had had more affairs while married than most men managed while single. He had even acknowledged the unwelcome spectre of his own womanising reputation with gritted teeth and conceded that as some excuse for Ione's refusal to immediately believe his side of the story on Pascale.

However, events had then taken a much more disturbing turn. Calling her security team to discover where she was, he had been appalled to realise that she had dismissed her bodyguards. Ione with that ridiculous attaché case packed full of cash and diamond jewellery was out *alone* and *unprotected*? Ione, who had no more idea of how to look after herself in the real world than a cartoon character?

He had been furious that he had not raised the subject of the contents of that case while they'd been in Paris! But he had been reluctant to hurt or embarrass her. After all, who did not have their little quirks? And if she could not bear to be parted from her late mother's hoard of jewellery and only felt secure with a vast amount of cash in her possession, where was the harm when she was guarded every place she went?

He had been on the brink of heading straight to the police when one of her bodyguards had admitted that she was actually being tailed by two of her team, but that, unsure whether he would have wished them to disobey her direct orders, their plea of initial ignorance had seemed wiser. His almost sick sense of relief had combined then with the first stirrings of an anger stronger and deeper than anything Alexio had ever felt in his life.

Awaiting a knock on the door of her suite, Ione stood taut, her head high, her chin at a defiant angle. It *had* to have been Alexio in that helicopter! She could not credit that coincidence could have brought one of his executives to the same country hotel. But beyond that level, her mind was in a loop. Even as she reminded herself that she was not afraid of anything that Alexio might say, panic and the most lowering sense of excitement were tearing her in two opposing directions.

No knock sounded. Instead there was a click as the card-entry mechanism was utilised and the door swung wide. Alexio powered in with his long, purposeful stride and the door thudded shut again in his wake. Golden eyes ablaze, his lean, strong face was rigid with forbidding constraint. Her heart banged up and down inside her like a ball being bounced on a very hard surface.

'How *dare* you register here as a Gakis?' Alexio launched at her without even pausing to gather his breath. 'How dare you deny my name?'

As an opening salvo, that was an unexpected one and Ione parted her lips, failed to think of anything cutting enough to say in response and closed her mouth again, keenest of all to retain her dignity.

'But then you have a remarkable degree of arrogance!'

Alexio shot at her in wrathful continuance. 'In that you are a Gakis right down to your little pearly fingertips!'

Green eyes widening, she stared back at him in genuine shock. 'That's not true—'

'Isn't it? What right did you have to tell me that our marriage was over? Are you the only person in this relationship? Are you always right and never wrong? Do you make a habit of judging others on the slightest of proof? Well, it's good to know that when our marriage hit its first minor storm, you baled out so fast you left a smoke trail!' Alexio completed with savage sarcasm.

Ione set her teeth together and refused to react.

'But then you're a Gakis…how could you possibly be wrong about anything?' Alexio punctuated that sardonic aside by setting a small disc recorder down on the dining table by the window. 'Only this time, as you're about to find out, you've made nothing but a bloody fool of yourself!'

'Really?' High spots of outraged pink had formed over Ione's cheekbones. 'What's that machine about to do? Paralyse me into stupidity?'

'*All* my office phone calls are recorded.' Alexio depressed the button with one stab of a long, punitive forefinger.

Ione stiffened as the disc began to play. She heard Alexio accepting the call from Pascale and the other woman's husky voice struck an immediate chord of recognition with her. She was surprised though to hear Pascale address Alexio in fluent Greek. Pascale announced that she was in London overnight and that, knowing that Alexio was in town as well, she was hoping that they could be together. As still as a marble image, her angry colour slowly draining away, Ione listened to the brief exchange that followed. The coolness edging Alexio's dark drawl was patent once he realised that Pascale had already made herself at home in the apartment, but the persistent brunette still tried to keep him chatting before suggesting a second time that he join her for dinner.

'Give me a break,' she heard Alexio say drily. 'Use the apartment tonight if you must but leave the key on your way out. I won't be visiting.'

'But you'll still know where to find me if you change your mind,' Pascale pointed out in a provocative purr before she rang off.

A deathly silence stretched then. Ione's hands continued to thread the loose ends of her sash back and forth between her restive fingers. Inside herself, she was coming apart at the seams with the craziest urge to shout and scream with joy and relief. She had been wrong, oh, yes, she had been very, very wrong and she was happy, indeed downright *ecstatic* to learn that she had misjudged her husband. The weight of sheer misery that she had been fighting off for endless hours fell from her in the space of an instant.

'Alexio…' Ione fixed shining eyes on him, her low-pitched voice hoarse with the fierceness of her emotions. 'I'm—'

'No.' Alexio lifted a lean, emphatic hand, shimmering golden eyes raking over her with contempt. 'Don't you dare to think for one moment that sorry is going to cut any ice with me *this* time around!'

Studying him with startled eyes, Ione breathed, 'But I *am* sorry—'

'You said you'd wait in that office but you *lied* to me. I've never stayed with a woman I can't trust. I also expect my wife to have the highest standards of loyalty and honesty. And you don't appear to have either quality!'

'But, I…' A thickness was blooming in Ione's throat

and clogging her vocal cords and she was so tense her muscles ached. She was devastated by that condemnation.

'No buts.' Lean, dark handsome face set hard, Alexio treated her to a raking head-to-toe appraisal that judged and found *her* wanting. 'You walked out on me when the very least you owed me was a hearing. At the first sign of trouble, you trashed everything we had and took off!'

'What was I supposed to believe when I found Pascale in your apartment?' Ione demanded emotively, her delicate bone structure drawn tight beneath her skin as she tried to defend herself.

'You were *supposed* to believe in me. You were *supposed* to value our marriage enough to stay and discuss the situation like an adult. But all you could think about was putting the boot in first and saving face,' Alexio derided. 'Nothing else mattered to you. You listened to nothing I said—'

'Pascale told me that you were lovers—'

'*Were* being the operative word. It's over two months since I last saw her and our casual arrangement ended well in advance of our wedding.'

'All right, I overreacted.' Desperation was beginning to get a strong grip on Ione. 'I should have given you more of a chance to explain…'

Alexio rested grim dark golden eyes on her. 'But that's not enough, is it? If Pascale had called me on my mobile phone, I wouldn't have been able to prove that I hadn't set up a meeting with her. But she didn't have my most recent number so she had to call me at the office. Where would we be now if I hadn't had a recording of that phone call?'

Ione turned bone-white as he floated that scenario before her.

'I think that without that recording I'd have been up

that four-letter word of a creek,' Alexio framed, his declaration raw-edged with bitter anger. 'If you can't have faith in me, we can't have a marriage.'

That tone of savage finality made Ione's heart sink to her toes. She had gone from ennervated defensiveness to soaring shame laced with joy, only to be cast down again. She had accused him of something he hadn't done and refused to trust his word. Indeed, she had been all too ready to believe him guilty. *Why?* she now asked herself in an agony of self-reproach. Why had she been so quick to judge him? She thought back to the glorious weeks they had shared in Paris and the high of happiness she had been on when she had arrived in London earlier that day. Dimly, she grasped what had gone wrong.

'You see...' Ione's voice emerged riven with strain...I'd never been so happy before and, perhaps, I couldn't quite believe in it. When Pascale said what she did, it was like I'd been expecting you to betray me all along. I just accepted it. It seemed much more realistic and familiar than all that happiness.'

Alexio was giving her an arrested look from beneath frowning black brows, his intense golden eyes locked to her, his big, powerful frame whip-taut with his growing tension as he listened.

'I think I'm very cynical. I don't think I'm arrogant. I think I try to protect myself because I've been hurt a lot,' Ione admitted in a tight undertone. 'I grew up in a home where my only strength was my pride, but I still had to sacrifice it to keep myself safe. I'm not accustomed to being able to depend on or trust anyone else but...but I can *learn.*'

Alexio endeavoured to conceal his shattered response to what she was telling him, but it was as though she had landed him a sudden hard punch in the stomach. He realised just how much his own contented and uncomplicated childhood had influenced his expectations of life and other people. He saw that what he had always taken for granted Ione had never had. Not the security, not the safety, not the trust that all needs would be met and definitely not the love. And that realisation just gutted him.

Closing the distance between them in a long stride, he hauled Ione into his arms. She stiffened in surprise but her heartbeat picked up speed like an express train. 'I don't want your pity—'

'Is lust OK?' Alexio broke in faster than the speed of light.

A ragged laugh escaped Ione. Suddenly pliant as a rag doll, she let him crush her close to his broad, muscular chest and squash her damp face into his shoulder. He smoothed her platinum-fair hair with a hand that wasn't quite steady and she registered that he was as shaken up as she was. 'I'm so sorry I put you through this,' she mumbled painfully.

'Forget it. I just realised that I was coming from a place you haven't got to yet,' Alexio delivered an assurance that she found incomprehensible in a wry undertone. 'But I didn't marry you to play around with other women. I've had years and years of total freedom to do whatever I liked and I *did* and I'm ready for something different now. You have to accept that too.'

'Yes…'

Someone knocked on the door and Alexio groaned. 'Who the hell is that?'

'It's probably the meal I ordered.'

Releasing her, Alexio opened the door. A waiter wheeled in a trolley, laid out the dishes and departed again with a very fat tip in his hand. Ione gazed at Alexio, every sense drinking him in: the brilliant, beautiful eyes that tied her in mental knots, the long, lithe strength and vitality of his lean, athletic frame, the supreme self-command that was as at home with blunt, open anger as affection and tenderness. He was a hell of a guy and she didn't feel she deserved him, didn't even know if he was willing to forgive her and didn't have the courage to ask.

Alexio lodged his intent gaze on her and the atmosphere sizzled. 'How hungry are you?' he enquired thickly.

'Not...' The instant that Ione recognised the smouldering flare of sexual hunger lighten his stunning eyes to pure mesmeric gold, her voice cried up on her and she couldn't find the rest of the words she needed.

But it seemed that Alexio understood for his slashing smile lightened the tension in his bronzed, masculine features. 'I want you too, *yineka mou*' he admitted, backing her step by step in the direction of the bedroom. 'You have no idea just how much.'

Relief cascaded through her and the breath caught in her throat. 'Still?'

'It's a round-the-clock obsession,' Alexio husked in hoarsened syllables as he reached for her and brought his mouth crashing down with raw passion on hers.

His sheer energy and unashamed need pulsed through Ione like an adrenalin charge. The explicit plunge and withdrawal of his tongue inside the tender interior of her mouth was so incredibly erotic that she whimpered helpless encouragement and clung to his shoulders, standing on tiptoes to aid him. With a rueful sound of frustration, Alexio lifted her off her feet and settled her down on the wide divan in the bedroom.

'I should still be mad with you,' he groaned. 'I don't chase all over the countryside after women. I don't *do* that kind of stuff—'

'You won't have to do it ever again,' Ione swore.

'You want to write that down and sign it in triplicate?' Alexio teased, capturing her lips in a long, drugging kiss that fired every fibre of her being while he extracted her from her robe with deft hands.

Wrenching himself back from her to undress, he rested molten eyes of appreciation on her. Ione lay there naked, face burning at the awareness that her nipples were visibly taut and swollen and that she ached for him.

'You're so beautiful,' Alexio breathed, coming back to her, all hard contours of powerful masculinity and over-whelmingly sexy.

He took her lush mouth again. He was all passion and plunder, ravishing her lips apart with his own, and she couldn't get enough of him, couldn't still the wild, trembling eagerness that had seized hold of her. She had thought they might never be together again and she ran her hands over his muscular arms, arched her spine up so that her tender breasts rubbed the hair-roughened wall of his chest, parted her thighs in instinctive invitation.

'Don't wait,' she muttered fiercely, letting her teeth graze a smooth, hard shoulder.

Alexio lifted his dark, tousled head, shimmering golden eyes ablaze with need and raw satisfaction. 'You want me that much?'

'Always…' she moaned as he discovered the slick, wet heat at the heart of her.

Slow and sure, he eased himself into her and the sensation was so intense that tears stung her eyes and her back arched in ecstasy. She strained up to him and sobbed out loud with frustration and excitement until his pagan rhythm matched her frantic fervour. The blinding instant of release convulsed her in a glorious overload of pleasure that sent shock waves splintering through her every skincell.

'I suppose I should let you eat now,' Alexio sighed with pronounced reluctance as he stole a last lingering kiss. He lifted her on top of him and closed his arms round her in a possessive hold that pinned her to every damp inch of his big, powerful frame. 'After all, I know that you haven't eaten since you stepped off the plane from Paris, *agape mou*.'

Brows pleating, Ione emerged from her somnolent daze of contentment to lift her tousled head. 'How do you know that?'

'You were tailed from my office. How do you think I found you so fast?' The teasing light in his gaze ebbed to be replaced by a more serious expression. 'Don't dismiss your bodyguards like that again.'

Ione coloured. 'If I was followed, they didn't listen to me.'

Alexio laced his hands into the wild tumble of her bright hair, level eyes censorious. 'I was very grateful they didn't listen. In Paris, you left that vanity case you take everywhere lying open one night in the dressing room and I *saw* the contents.'

Ione froze and lost every scrap of natural colour. He had actually seen the money that had once figured as her escape fund from their marriage? She had had no idea how to dispose of that money without running the risk of alerting Alexio to the reality that her flight on their wedding day had been a pre-planned event.

'That cash ought to be in the bank and the diamonds should be in a safe,' Alexio murmured gently.

Dry-mouthed, Ione nodded in instant agreement and fearfully waited for him to ask the obvious question of why she had found it necessary to carry round a case stuffed with money and her late mother's jewellery. But Alexio just smiled, that heart-stopping smile that always left her weak with love. Almost as weak with relief that he had not enquired further into the matter, Ione buried her discomfited face in his shoulder, her guilty conscience weighing heavy. She would never be able to confess the truth. If he ever found out how selfish and foolish she had been before their wedding, he would not forgive her.

'So…' Alexio drawled with studied casualness. 'You called at a house before you checked in here. What was that about?'

Ione grinned, her attack of conscience falling to the back of her mind as she thought about her twin. 'That house belonged to my twin's foster mother. I said who I was and *now*…I've got Misty's phone number!'

Alexio sat up in a sudden movement that took her by surprise. 'What did your sister say when you called?'

'I haven't called yet…I thought it was too late at night—'

Alexio unleashed a groan and made her tell him exactly what she had said and to whom at Fossetts. 'Don't you realise that your twin's probably sitting by the phone right now *waiting* for that call? People don't keep information like that to themselves. I'm sure she's already been told that you went to her foster mum's home and got her number.'

Ione reddened. 'I'll call first thing in the morning.'

Vaulting out of bed, Alexio strode into the sitting room to retrieve the piece of paper he had noted earlier lying on the coffee-table. He was amused at himself. Why on earth had he got the crazy idea that that might be Yannis's number? The fisherman's son was old history.

Minutes later, Ione found herself seated with a phone planted into her hand while her husband stood by, his magnificent body interrupted only by a pair of grey jersey boxer shorts. 'It's after midnight,' she protested tautly. 'It's just not right to call this late.'

'You're scared and she's probably scared too. Get on with it,' Alexio instructed.

The phone was answered by a breathless female voice even before Ione heard it ring at her end of the line. 'I'm Ione Christoulakis,' she said unsteadily. Is that Misty?'

'Yes. Are you my twin?' the voice asked anxiously.

'Yes. I don't know what to say to you...now I've found you—'

'My head's in a spin too. In fact, I'm thrilled to death. I was terrified you weren't going to call and I couldn't *believe* that Birdie's cousin had let you go without even getting your name or your address!' Misty's voice had gathered steam and pace to become bright and excited. 'If we arrange a special flight for you, will you fly up here tonight?'

Ione's eyes rounded in astonishment and she turned to speak to Alexio in Greek.

'No,' he pronounced at decisive speed. 'You're already on the edge of exhaustion. Tell her, we'll fly up early tomorrow morning.'

'Who are you with?' Misty asked with intense curiosity. 'And what is that language you're speaking?'

And from that point on, all awareness vanished. While Alexio ordered fresh meals for them both on the hotel's internal phone, Ione curled up on the sofa and rushed to answer her twin's surge of eager questions before finally gaining the confidence to press her own. Alexio went for a shower. Supper arrived and Ione ate it with one hand in tiny morsels because she couldn't stop talking. Only when it got to the point where she was smothering yawns through every sentence did she reach the stage where she could face saying goodbye to her twin for a few hours.

Then she just slumped with a dazed and happy smile on her weary mouth. 'My sister lives in a castle,' she informed Alexio.

Alexio lifted his wife off the sofa, carried her through to the bedroom and slotted her between the sheets. Even in the time it took him to reappear with the rings he had scooped off the coffee-table, and which he had steadfastly desisted from commenting on, she had gone out like a light into a deep sleep. He threaded her wedding ring back onto her limp hand and then wondered why it had seemed so important to do that.

By the time the helicopter landed the following day at the private airstrip at Castle Eyrie, Ione was bubbling over with a heady mixture of excitement and nerves.

'Misty's going to love you,' Alexio forecast, enclosing Ione's taut fingers in a reassuring hold as he helped her climb out. 'You got on like a house on fire on the phone last night.'

All Ione's attention centred on the woman hurrying towards them and the big smile of welcoming warmth on her twin's vibrant face.

'Let me look at you...' Copper hair streaming back from her brow in the breeze, Misty bounded up with the lithe grace of her very long legs, bright silver-grey eyes engaged in a fascinated appraisal of her smaller, tenser twin. 'Oh, my goodness, you're tiny...and really, *really* beautiful,' she gasped, slowly shaking her head. 'Our gene pool was a real lucky bag. But you're the living image of our paternal grandmother. Our father has a portrait of her. She was a legendary beauty in the thirties.'

And as Ione met her sister's emotive gaze and saw the tears there that mirrored her own and heard those words, which for the very first time connected her to another family, her heart felt as if it were ballooning inside her. She didn't know who made the move first but they engulfed each other in a clumsy hug, laughing and crying at the same time. Then Misty's arm wrapped round her, Ione was urged over to a sports car, tucked into the passenger seat and wafted back to the castle with her chattering sister at the wheel.

Meanwhile, Leone and Alexio had been introducing themselves, standing back at a distance, striving not to spoil that special moment when their respective wives saw each other for the first time in over twenty years.

'Bloody hell...' Leone breathed in disbelief as the car sped past about thirty feet away. 'Misty's stranded us!'

Silence reigned for several seconds while both men waited for the car to slacken speed and turn. Alexio and Leone exchanged a brief glance of mutual male incredulity, but neither felt it necessary to remark on the fact that they had been overlooked like left luggage in the general excitement.

They strolled back to the castle and Leone broke the news that there was yet another sister called Freddy. A half-sister, born of Ione's natural mother's first marriage and married to the Crown Prince of Quamar. 'She talks a lot too,' Leone commented. 'And Misty was on the phone to her at dawn today, so I suspect you're going to be meeting Freddy soon as well.'

'The more the merrier,' Alexio quipped with easy amusement. 'Ione doesn't have much in the way of family.'

'Minos Gakis?' Acknowledging that he was already aware of exactly *who* Ione was, Leone absorbed Alexio's momentarily grim expression and relaxed a little more. 'I suggest we go for lunch—'

'Leave them to their reunion, stay out late.' An appre-

ciative smile formed on Alexio's wide, shapely mouth.
'Just how long do you think it'll take our wives to miss
us?'

Curled up at either end of the same sofa in the lofty drawing room and sharing a pot of coffee, Misty and Ione only
remembered the husbands they had abandoned when
Murdo, the elderly butler, came in to announce lunch and
asked if his employer and Mr Christoulakis would be back
in time for the meal. Aghast expressions crossed Ione's
and Misty's faces at the exact same moment. They met
each other's eyes and then went off into a guilty fit of
giggles at what they had done.

'Have you ever forgotten about Leone before?' Ione
whispered chokily.

'No, and I bet he's furious,' Misty groaned. 'What about
Alexio?'

'I wouldn't think it would have made his day,' Ione
confided, but, learning from Murdo that their husbands had
returned to the castle and departed from there in Leone's
four-wheel drive, the sisters relaxed again. The first part
of the day had passed with Ione keen to hear her sister
describe their late mother and learn about Carrie Carlton's
ill-starred affair with their natural father, Oliver Sargent.
She'd been truly thrilled at the news that she still had
another older sister, Freddy, to meet. But the afternoon
passed with the simple pleasure of cradling her adorable
little nephew, Connor, on her lap and just talking and getting to know her twin.

That evening, Ione stood at their Gothic bedroom window in the castle watching the sun go down over the shimmering loch and released a wondering sigh of contentment.
Alexio, who had reappeared with Leone just in time for
what had proved to be a very entertaining dinner, tugged

her into his arms and turned her round to face him. 'Good day?'

She looked up into his spectacular eyes and, acknowledging how very special he was, she just melted from outside him. 'Heavenly.'

'We should buy a house over here.'

Ione tensed and then, appreciating that it was past time that she practised greater openness with Alexio, she took a deep breath. 'We don't need to. I inherited Cosmas's London townhouse and my adoptive mother left me Caradore Park, her family's country home. I haven't visited either property but my father makes use of both when he's in England.'

Lean, strong face clenching hard, Alexio was very still. 'And you didn't consider those facts worth mentioning before now?'

Ione evaded his incredulous gaze and contrived a shrug. 'It just didn't seem important. You know…I think I'll go for a bath,' she muttered in the sizzling silence, heading for the *en suite* at supersonic speed.

Alexio drew in a slow, deep sustaining breath. He caught the bathroom door before it could snap shut. 'There's more, *isn't* there?'

Taut as a bowstring, Ione gulped. 'Mama and Cosmas left me everything.'

One glance at Alexio's rigidity was sufficient to assure Ione that her husband had a very good idea of what everything encompassed and an awful silence stretched while he absorbed that revelation.

'So…' Alexio drawled with noticeably flat diction. 'You place it all in trust for our children.'

The silence fell thick and quiet again.

'No…' Ione almost whispered.

Glittering golden eyes backed by all the force of

Alexio's powerful personality locked to her. 'I've already given you my views on this subject.'

Paling at that fair and true reminder, Ione bent her head.

'Every Greek husband regards it as his right to provide for his wife,' Alexio declared with stubborn conviction.

His ferocious pride was getting in the way of his intelligence, Ione reflected with gritted teeth. She could not credit that his partnership with her father would last the course and she was trying to protect them both. Sooner or later, Minos Gakis would do something underhanded in business that would alienate Alexio. When Alexio attempted to dissolve that partnership, her father would try to destroy him. A time might come when even Alexio might appreciate that advantage of not having a dependent wife whose wealth was tied up for posterity in trust funds.

'I won't compromise on this score,' Alexio warned her with a lethal quiet assurance that sent a shiver down her slender spine. 'It is a matter of what is *right*.'

As he shut the door on her again with a definitive snap, she jerked and accidentally up-ended an entire dish of fragrant bath bombs into the tub. They fizzed like noisy fireworks sending out a rainbow of streaking colours that blurred beneath her fraught gaze. So much for honesty!

By the time she emerged Alexio was in bed, lying back against the banked-up pillows, one long, powerful thigh exposed by the covers he had disarranged. Shimmering golden eyes locked to her and her mouth ran dry, heart jumping, pulses speeding up. The sheer, gorgeous impact of him continually knocked her flat and left her breathless.

'As I see it, *agape mou*,' Alexio murmured levelly, 'this too is a matter of trust. Do you or do you not have faith in my ability to look after you?'

Instantly, Ione saw the drawbacks of having allowed that keen, cutting intellect of his the space to come up with the most devastating argument available to him. 'How can you be so low as to ask me that? What can I say to such a question?'

'*Yes…*or…*no*?' Alexio traded, refusing to back down an inch.

Aware that even a hint of a negative on that score would outrage his pride and undermine their marriage, Ione did something she had never done before: she slid with the most seductive wriggle she had ever contrived out of her nightdress. She felt the sudden sexual burn of Alexio's intent gaze on her pouting breasts and slim hips, the sudden instant shift in atmosphere that resulted as his all-too-potent virility focused him on earthier pleasures. Barely breathing and her face hot, she sauntered over to the bed and got in beside him, arching her back as she shook her silvery mane of hair back off her narrow shoulders.

'Yes…of course, yes,' she whispered sweetly.

'You're a witch,' Alexio growled, scorching golden eyes flaring over her exquisite face as he locked one hand into her glorious hair. Hauling her caveman-style down on top of him, he locked his hungry mouth to hers and claimed a fiery kiss that currented through her quivering length with the efficiency of a heat-seeking missile.

Over the weekend that followed at the castle, Ione talked to her half-sister, Freddy, at length on the phone and agreed to meet up with her natural father, Oliver, for lunch on her next visit to London. It was time for her and Alexio to return to Greece and, although she knew it would be a wrench to leave her twin behind, she could bear that better than she could have borne being parted from Alexio. Their marriage was too new and she was far too much in love to accept Misty's invitation to stay on at the castle without Alexio for another few days.

Minutes before Alexio and Ione embarked on their flight

to Athens, Alexio received an urgent call that he took in private. Only after the jet had taken off did Ione notice the lines of tension holding his lean, darkly handsome features taut and the sombre look in his gaze.

'What's wrong?' she asked.

Alexio released his breath in a slow, pent-up hiss. Shock was still coursing through him. He had just received the news that his father-in-law's condition had, with very little warning, worsened. His doctors had decided that the planned surgery was now out of the question and that there was little more they could do for him. Assailed by the total innocence of Ione's enquiring gaze, he cursed his own reluctance to break his word to Minos.

'Ione…your father is seriously ill,' he imparted.

Before his eyes, Ione's face went white. 'Since…since when?'

Alexio closed his hands round hers and told her exactly what her father had told him over six weeks earlier.

CHAPTER NINE

HER shattered expression a clear indication of the level of her shock, Ione dragged her fingers from Alexio's in a driven jerky movement. 'Papa is dying…and you *knew* and you kept that from me?'

''It was your father's wish that neither you nor your aunt were told. He was to have surgery in a few weeks. Now that's not an option,' Alexio conceded tautly while Ione continued to stare at him with accusing and stricken eyes. 'But I believed, as Minos believed, that the crisis point was still some time away.'

'The crisis point…' Ione trembled, spun away from him like an uncoordinated doll. She remembered that her father had looked ill when he had come home from his last trip abroad, but she had put that down to overwork for he had always driven himself too hard. How could she *not* have realised? How could Alexio *not* have warned her?

'I believed that I still had plenty of time in which to prepare you,' Alexio admitted with audible regret.

'And you are the man who *dared* to tell me that I did not meet your standards of honesty?' Ione slung at him with quivering force, lashing out wildly at him because she was being eaten alive by guilt. Guilt that she had been so absorbed in her own problems months earlier that she had neglected to note her father's declining health. Guilt that she had so recently planned to leave the Gakis family for ever in a manner that would have caused her father immense public embarrassment and annoyance.

'I did not like to break my word to him.' Making that

admission in a driven undertone, Alexio spread speaking, fluid hands in an expressive movement that was wholly Greek.

'So even Papa has more rights in this marriage than I do!' Ione hurled at him, taking off on another tangent without skipping a beat. 'You put your word to him above your loyalty to me, but this is a *family* issue…and you are *not* a Gakis!'

Shaking like a leaf, Ione collapsed down into her seat. She could not look at him because she knew that what she was saying was unfair. He knew too well what her home life had been like. But, for the first time in many years, Ione was registering that, in spite of everything, she cared for her father, could not *help* caring for her father, could not think of herself as anything other than Greek and a Gakis because that was where her earliest remembered roots were and always would be. Finding her twin, Misty, had filled her with joy, but she had felt oddly detached from their discussions about their natural parents and only now did she appreciate why that had been so: twenty-three years of living another life could not be set aside or overlooked.

'You'll be on Lexos by this evening,' Alexio assured her.

With difficulty, Ione swallowed the ballooning thickness in her throat. 'Papa hates to be fussed over. I understand why he chose not to tell me or Kalliope about his condition. It's not your fault.'

In the early hours of the following morning, Ione left her father's room where only medical personnel now held sway. Her father had been so ill that throughout the hours she had sat by his bedside he had not once seemed aware of her presence. Seeing the parent who had always dominated the household in such a weak state had been a considerable shock for Ione. No, there would be no improvement, the doctor had informed her: the older man had suffered a major heart attack.

Conscious that it was too late to go and talk to her aunt, who was so distraught over her brother's condition that she had yet to emerge from her rooms to speak to either Alexio or her niece, Ione went back to her own suite. It had been several hours since she had seen Alexio for her father's lawyers, in company with his top executives, had been anxiously awaiting her husband's arrival at the villa. Alexio was now in official charge of the Gakis empire and Ione was painfully aware that the demands on both his time and his attention would be immense.

As she entered her sitting room she was surprised to see the doors spread back on the balcony, and then her heart quickened when she saw Alexio there, his jacket and tie discarded and his formal shirt open at his strong brown throat.

'I thought you'd still be working…'

'Not when I have to start work again in a few hours' time, *agape mou.*' Alexio held out his arms in an expansive motion that made her strained eyes sting with tears. She hurtled into that embrace like a homing pigeon.

'And then how could I go to bed without first pausing to admire your teddy-bear collection in the moonlight?' Alexio remarked deadpan, casting meaningful eyes at the room a few feet away where the bears sat around on display.

A chokey little laugh escaped Ione at that sally. She loved him so much that sometimes it almost hurt to be that close to him. Weak at the knees, she curved into his big, powerful frame, taking strength from the warmth and strength of his hard, muscular body, drowning in the husky, familiar scent of his skin. 'Cosmas was planning to have cabinets built for them—'

'A most indulgent brother.'

Ione looked up at him with rueful green eyes. 'I like bears but it was Cosmas who was totally crazy about them.'

A pleat formed between Alexio's winged ebony brows. *'Cosmas?'*

With a sigh, Ione murmured, 'He was gay…'

Taken aback, Alexio stared down at her with astonished dark golden eyes.

'Another Gakis secret known to very few,' Ione conceded with wry acceptance.

'Did Minos know?'

'Of course not. Papa was always telling Cosmas to find a wife.' In the moonlight, the pale, perfect triangle of Ione's face shadowed at that memory. 'The last few months of his life, Cosmas was under enormous strain, but he couldn't face telling Papa the truth.'

'I can imagine what a challenge that would have been.'

'In different ways,' Ione breathed in a wobbly undertone, her full mouth tremulous, 'both I and Cosmas were great disappointments to Papa…and now when I *see* him so—'

'Shush.' Alexio's strong arms tightened round her. 'Losing someone else always brings guilty feelings to the surface but what is done is done. Had I accepted that sooner, I would've dealt better with Crystal's death. But instead I blamed myself for what happened to her.'

Ione tensed in surprise at that admission. 'But why?'

Alexio lounged in a fluid motion back against the wrought-iron balustrade. His lean features were taut, black lashes low over his reflective golden gaze. 'Crystal and I had a row the day she died.' His expressive mouth compressed. 'She wanted me to set a date for the wedding and I refused. We'd had the same argument on several occasions. But that particular night we were staying in a beachside villa on Corfu—'

Ione studied his lean, dark, devasting features with keen interest. 'Why wouldn't you set a date?'

'During one of our many periods apart, she slept with another guy.' Alexio pushed long brown fingers through his luxuriant black hair and shifted a wide shoulder, his jawline squaring as Ione failed to conceal her disconcertion at that blunt revelation. 'Although I still wanted to *be* with her, I couldn't forget that. Our guests on Corfu were her friends. They liked to drink and horse around pretty much round the clock and I was bored. I left them and went off to work in another room. I never saw her alive again.'

Ione swallowed hard and touched his arm in an awkward movement, needing to show her sympathy but unable to find adequate words.

'A crowd of them went for a midnight swim. By the time they realised that Crystal was missing, it was too late. I felt like I'd *killed* her,' Alexio admitted with a quiet, charged force that shook Ione.

'*No…*' Ione breathed fiercely, closing her arms round him in turn and finally understanding why it had taken so long for him to get over Crystal Denby. Guilt. He had blamed himself for that final argument and for not being there in the water when his fiancée had needed him. 'It was a horrible accident…it was the same as Cosmas crashing his plane. There was nothing anybody could have done to prevent it.'

'But I'd never have let her go swimming after she'd been drinking. That *is* a fact,' Alexio countered ruefully.

'However, I don't beat myself up about it any more. Crystal often took crazy risks and rarely heeded advice.'

Tensing, Ione worried at her full lower lip. 'I must seem very dull stuff after her...'

'Are you kidding?' Vibrant amusement flashed through Alexio's stunning eyes and, throwing his proud, dark head back, he laughed with rich appreciation. 'I never know what you're going to do next!'

Colour warmed her cheeks. 'I won't ever walk out on our marriage again.'

'I don't plan to give you cause, *agape mou*.' With a husky sound low in his throat, Alexio captured her lips with sweet, delicious expertise and the anguished insecurities that had tormented her throughout the previous day fell into abeyance for what remained of the night.

Ione was up by eight and by then Alexio's side of the bed was already empty. Having talked to the doctor watching over her father and learned that there was no change, she went for breakfast.

Kalliope was already seated at the table in the superb panelled dining room. As Ione greeted her the older woman dealt her a resentful look and two highspots of pink marked her thin cheeks. 'So *at last* you are gracing us with your attention.'

'Had I known that Papa was ill, I would have come home sooner,' Ione protested.

Kalliope pursed her lips. 'You're lying. Don't lie to me.'

One glance was sufficient to warn Ione that her aunt was in a more than usually difficult mood. A look of sincere bewilderment on her face, Ione tensed in receipt of that condemnation, but she said nothing for she had no wish to be drawn into a hostile exchange with the older woman.

On the threshold of the room and unobserved by either

woman, however, Alexio came to a halt when he heard that same accusation. A censorious light in his gaze, he frowned at Kalliope Gakis.

All Kalliope's attention was centred on her niece. 'I spoke to Tipo after your husband dispensed with his services in Paris. I found out that you walked out on your marriage only a few hours after the wedding—'

Belatedly understanding exactly what her aunt was getting at, Ione jerked and lost colour and began talking fast in her own defence. 'That was all sorted out. I made a very foolish mistake but Alexio and I are happy together now.'

'A mistake? Is that what you call it?' The Greek woman raised an unimpressed brow. 'I let Tipo complete his investigation. He discovered that you booked that flight to London a full nine days *before* you even married Alexio Christoulakis!'

In the act of striding forward to draw attention to his presence, Alexio switched his attention to Ione at supersonic speed. 'Is this true?' he demanded of his wife before he had even allowed himself to absorb the full meaning of what he had just overheard.

The glass in Ione's hand tipped between her suddenly nerveless fingers and spilt a puddle of orange juice onto the polished surface of the dining table. While a gasp of dismay erupted from her aunt at Alexio's sudden appearance, Ione felt like someone frozen in time and space. Paralysed with horror at the knowledge that her husband had heard Kalliope's accusation, she stared across the room entrapped by Alexio's stunned dark golden eyes.

'I believe I asked you a question,' Alexio breathed with lethal quietness.

Pushing her chair back, Kalliope stood up. Her aghast scrutiny flickering between her niece's shattered face and

Alexio's menacing stillness, she muttered a stifled apology and hurried out of the room.

Ione set down her glass with a trembling hand and rose unsteadily upright. 'Alexio—'

'Shut up,' Alexio incised, cutting and quiet as a rapier blade. 'You know what I am asking you. Is it true that you booked that London flight nine days *before* our wedding?'

The hideous silence clawed at Ione's nerves for she did not know how to respond. Yes, it was the truth, but it was an appalling truth that might destroy their relationship. If she gave that confirmation, she would be admitting that she had agreed to marry him solely to use him and their wedding as a means of escape from her father's domination. She would be confessing that she had *never* intended to be his real wife, *never* intended even to live with him. And to make such a confession now when they had found such happiness was more than Ione could bear.

Torn apart by fear of the consequences, she gazed back at him, her skin clammy, her heart sinking like a stone. His superb bone structure was prominent beneath his bronzed skin, ferocious tension etched into the hard line of his mouth and his strong jaw as he waited for the response that she would have given ten years of her life at that moment to avoid.

'I'll ask you one last time…' Alexio breathed with raw emphasis. 'Is it the truth?'

Ione's rigid shoulders slumped as she recognised the complete impossibility of sidestepping that leading question. Pale as milk and trembling, she parted bloodless lips and muttered heavily, 'Yes. I wish I could say it was a ghastly lie but unhappily for me…it *is* the truth…'

In the depths of his brilliant dark golden eyes she saw all that she had feared: shock, incredulous disgust but,

worst of all, she saw his angry pain that she could have
sunk that low, cared so little for his feelings, indeed considered nobody but her own self. That single lancing look
was the very worst punishment he could have given her
and it filled her with the most terrible guilt and remorse
she had ever experienced.

'It was wrong…but at the time, I was desperate. Papa
hadn't allowed me to leave the island for four years. I was
like a prisoner here,' she reasoned sickly, her agonised
gaze clinging to his lean, hard features and the pallor
spreading round his taut mouth. 'I wasn't thinking straight.
I wasn't capable of thinking about how my plans would
affect you—'

'Or even caring?' Alexio slotted in lethally.

Pained colour flared in her cheekbones. 'It was selfish
and stupid and I regret that I ever thought that way—'

'You went through our wedding *knowing* what you were
planning to do…' Alexio loosed a ragged laugh of disbelief, viewing her with renewed recoil. 'How could you
do that? How could you go into that church and lie as you
took the same vows that I took in faith and sincerity? Is
there no end to the deception you're capable of?'

'I changed my mind at the last minute—'

'You changed your mind because I confronted you,'
Alexio countered with harsh clarity.

'No…even before you found me at the airport, I had
already had second thoughts about what I was doing!' Ione
argued feverishly. 'I felt terrible. I couldn't bring myself
to leave you—'

'Maybe the thought of that big wide world of freedom
was a little too threatening for you by that stage. I don't
accept that belated loyalty or decency had *any* sway over
your behaviour. And we'll never know whether or not you
would have got on that flight, will we?' Alexio pointed

out in the same fierce tone of condemnation, his lean, powerful face grim and hard.

'I already had feelings for you…and I was f-fighting them!' Ione stammered in increasing turmoil. She could see the way the dialogue was going. He had just given her a frightening glimpse of how complete was his loss of faith in her.

His beautiful eyes as dark as the midnight hour, he viewed her with fierce condemnation. 'You just used me like I was nothing on your terms. Well, you have now proved to my full satisfaction that you require no blood bond to be a Gakis through and through…for only a Gakis would act with such total disregard for others!'

Her gaze lowering from his in shame and turmoil, Ione flinched for she could not excuse herself. Her original intention to use their marriage to her own ends had been indefensible and she had abandoned her escape plan too late to impress him. Had she turned back before she'd returned to the airport in Paris on their wedding day, it might have made a difference to his outlook, but she had not.

'I deserve that but I *couldn't* tell you the truth afterwards—'

'Had you admitted the truth that day at the airport hotel, I would have let you go,' Alexio interrupted with cold, brutal conviction. 'Our marriage would've been annulled. Indeed nothing on this earth would have persuaded me to give you a second chance!'

Ione tried and failed to swallow and mumbled unevenly, 'I very much wanted that second chance, Alexio.'

He shook his proud dark head in slow motion. 'I can't credit what a fool I've been! Your behaviour at our wedding…the cash and the jewellery in your luggage…the weakness of your excuses. I actually told myself I was dealing with a nervous virgin. I was ready and willing to be suckered. Do you know why?'

In sick dread of what he might say next, Ione shook her own head.

'No woman had ever ditched me before and at least a dozen women had tried to get me to the altar,' Alexio confided with seething self-derision stamped into his devastatingly handsome features. 'I was prepared to believe any excuse sooner than credit the ego-zapping truth: the woman I had chosen to make my wife, the woman I expected to grow old beside, was happy to walk out on our marriage a few hours after the ceremony!'

Despair was building in Ione by the second. 'Don't judge me for what I did weeks ago when I hardly knew you,' she pleaded. 'I'm not the same person any more and our marriage is the most important thing in my life now. I *care* about you—'

'So much that a mere hint of infidelity made you abandon our relationship a second time,' Alexio incised with lethal timing.

That destructive and dangerous reminder sent a wave of desperation travelling through Ione. Nothing she had said seemed to have made the smallest impression on him. In addition, Kalliope's revelation was now encouraging Alexio to put an even more damaging slant on more recent events.

Alexio spread two lean hands in a curiously clumsy movement that lacked his usual fluid grace. 'Our relationship is a lie...' he murmured in a roughened undertone. 'All of it right from the beginning—'

'No...no, it wasn't!' Ione cut in frantically.

Alexio cast her a look of murderous reproach. 'Are you seriously asking me to believe now that you ever had a photo of me in your locker at school?'

And it was with that unsettling and least expected final comment that Alexio strode out of the room. Ione slumped down into her chair, buried her face in her hands and sobbed her heart out. She was trying not to think of how many times she had stolen a look at those pin-up pics of Alexio over her classmate's shoulder.

Some minutes later, she jerked when someone squeezed her shoulder in a brief, awkward gesture of sympathy. Lifting her head, she was disconcerted to see her aunt looking down at her with guilty concern.

'I didn't mean to cause trouble between you and your husband,' Kalliope declared tautly. 'I like Alexio. He is part of the family now. I was angry with you. But I *wouldn't* have spoken had I known he was there to hear.'

'I know,' Ione conceded heavily.

Kalliope nodded in her more usual brisk manner, her relief that her niece had not chosen to make more of an issue of the matter palpable. 'Then let us both go and sit with your father now.'

Minos Gakis passed away late that afternoon. Alexio came to Ione within minutes and said and did everything that might have been expected of him. Kalliope collapsed into his arms in tears. Ione was grateful for his support, but painfully conscious of the shuttered look in his brilliant gaze and the new distance she sensed in him. She hoped to talk to him that evening, but Kalliope's extreme distress, the arrangements for the private funeral and the demands of business all intervened. When Ione finally fell into bed exhausted that night, Alexio was still working, and when she woke up the next morning only the dent in the pillow beside hers was evidence that he had shared the same bed at some stage of the night.

Later that day, Alexio joined his wife and her aunt for lunch. There was no opportunity for private conversation and Ione could not help wondering if that had been why Alexio had chosen to put in an appearance at the table. She could not approach him in the office suite where he was surrounded by staff. Her troubled eyes fixed to his lean dark face as she strove to fathom what was going on inside his head and whether or not it was perhaps wiser for her not to force another discussion at such a stressful time. And what more could she say that she had not already said? Yet how could she remain silent when every passing hour seemed to be deepening the distance between them?

When Alexio had not returned to their room by midnight that same evening, Ione could stand being without him no longer. Scrambling out of bed, she pulled on a hand-painted floral silk robe and set off for the office wing. She found Alexio so deep in work at her father's giant desk that he did not even register her quiet approach.

For a moment, Ione just hovered, feasting her hungry eyes on his hard, bronzed profile, the lush darkness of his lashes as he scrolled down the page on the laptop computer he was using, the luxuriant black hair that gleamed in the lamp light. Thinking of how he had once accused her of baling out of their marriage at the first sign of trouble, she straightened her already taut shoulders. She did not want to lose him. Indeed the mere thought of losing Alexio terrified her.

'Are you coming to bed soon?' Ione enquired stiltedly, sheer nervous tension working on her vocal cords and drying her mouth.

Alexio glanced up, dark golden eyes shielded by his spiky lashes. Thrusting back his chair, he rose with innate good manners to his full commanding height. 'I doubt it. Your father's lawyers wish to read his will tomorrow and they require these figures.'

'Couldn't someone else do it?'

'I'm afraid not. I mean no offence,' Alexio murmured levelly, 'but the most senior executives in the Gakis empire couldn't tie their own shoelaces without a direct order.'

Ione coloured. 'Papa liked to stay in control.'

'Yes, but it does leave me, in the short term, without a normal company infrastructure to rely on,' Alexio pointed out in the same even tone.

He was speaking to her in the same courteous, reasonable manner he had utilised since the previous day. Not as he had once spoken to her with warmth and intimacy. Her heart ached inside her and her eyes burned with unshed tears. 'Are you ever going to forgive me?'

His strong dark features set and unreadable golden eyes met hers in the briefest of collisions. 'What is there to forgive?' he enquired. 'I have a very good idea of what your life was once like. You were powerless and you chose the only means at your disposal to seize the chance of another life—'

'But at what cost now to *us*?' Ione broke in emotively, troubled rather than relieved by that logical concession. 'You're telling me that you understand *why* I did what I did but that's not what I asked—'

'I said there was nothing to forgive,' Alexio reminded her. 'You made a rational decision and, in your position then, I might have done the same myself. Ethics really don't enter the equation when it comes to survival.'

Ione was so tense that her legs had begun shaking. 'Right from the start, I was drawn to you but I fought it every step of the way. I wouldn't allow myself to trust you…I wouldn't let myself *think* about what I was doing to you—'

'I don't think we need to talk about this.'

She focused on his strong, stubborn jawline where a bluish shadow of stubble was already visible and she could have wept. She had hurt his pride, destroyed his trust in her and shattered their marriage and yet he was standing there evading the issue with a determination that shook her.

'But one matter I should mention…' Alexio continued in his cool, measured drawl. 'I was wrong to ask you to put your wealth into trust funds for our children. I had no right whatsoever to demand such a sacrifice and in retrospect it does seem rather ridiculous—'

'No, it wasn't ridiculous,' Ione interrupted chokily, ready to sign away all that she possessed at that instant if it would heal the giant, terrifying chasm that had opened up between them.

'Of course it was.' Alexio dealt her a weary, mocking smile that turned her inside out with anguished regret. 'Tomorrow, you will become one of the richest women in the world.'

'What is mine is yours,' Ione protested in despair.

'I signed up to take care of the Gakis empire and profit only through my partnership with your father. Now that he is gone, I will take nothing that is yours,' Alexio imparted with quiet dignity.

'If that's going to become another barrier between us, I'll *give* it all away!' Ione threatened wildly.

Alexio expelled his breath in a stark hiss of censure that shrivelled her where she stood. 'You have a duty of care and responsibility towards many thousands of employees. If the Gakis empire is broken up, the asset strippers will move in and there will be huge redundancies.'

As Ione gazed back at him in visible dismay, Alexio added, 'I think you should also take into account the reality that you might find being poor something of a challenge.'

Catching the slight quiver in his dark, deep drawl, Ione recognised the sudden amusement he was struggling to conceal, for of course what she had said had been foolish. As it was the first crack she had seen in his disturbing detachment, she took strength from it.

'I'll wait up for you.' Ione backed towards the door as she made that breathless promise. 'And, by the way, those pin-ups of you might not have been in *my* school locker but I often took a sneaky look at them!'

At that leading reference to his own bitter words the day before, Alexio went rigid. Shimmering golden eyes lit on her with all the angry turmoil he had worked so hard to conceal from her, but then lingered to make an almost involuntary appraisal of her tumbling silvery blonde hair and the lissom, feminine curves enhanced by fine silk. For a split second as she collided with his intent gaze the atmosphere was electric with an excitement that fired her every skincell and she trembled. Then the phone buzzed and the moment was lost as he swung away to answer it.

Heart beating very fast, Ione returned to bed. He still wanted her, didn't he? Well, she wasn't too proud to take advantage of that chink in his armour. Maybe she ought to have thrown herself across his desk there and then. Or maybe she ought just to have told him how much she loved and needed him.

But in the end all those frantic, feverish thoughts proved to be a waste of time and energy for when dawn broke the skies Ione was still alone and in an even more distraught frame of mind than she had been earlier. Alexio had ignored her unspoken invitation. Alexio, who had never, ever said no to her, had rejected her for the first time. In turmoil, Ione started wondering if he was planning

to divorce her once he had dealt with all the vast complications of her father's estate. Might that explain why he
had been so careful to state that he would not profit in any
way from anything that was hers?

CHAPTER TEN

'WHAT would *I* have done in your position?' Misty mused reflectively on the phone to Ione a week later. 'I think I would've lied like a trooper.'

'Misty...' Ione groaned.

'There are some things that men are just not equipped to deal with,' her twin informed her with complete cool. 'Admitting that you planned to desert him within hours of taking your marriage vows *definitely* falls into that category! Alexio is a real romantic...don't you appreciate that? He greeted you with flowers on the church steps on your wedding day. He thought it was sweet that you fancied him as a schoolgirl. I think it's time you told him how you really feel about him.'

'I told him how *much* I cared—

'I care about lots of people but I don't *love* them. Alexio's been spoiled by women most of his life and then he got hitched to you and, since then, *he's* been the one doing the spoiling!'

'Yes,' Ione acknowledge thickly, her throat closing over with the threat of tears. 'But he's been away so much on business, I've hardly seen him this week and I know that that is not his fault but it's not helping matters.'

Misty sighed. 'I just wish you'd let Freddy and I fly over for the funeral. We could've given you support and talked so much better face to face.'

'I was fine and I'm still fine,' Ione had observed the wishes that Minos Gakis had expressed in his will and only a tiny handful of his closest surviving relatives had attended the event. Although she would have loved to have invited her sisters, she had also had to consider Kalliope's likely reaction to the presence of strangers at such a time.

When Ione had finally relinquished the comfort of talking her problems round in circles with the outspoken sister whom she was already beginning to think of as a best friend, she walked out onto the glorious flower-decked balcony beyond her new sitting room. In one brief week so many changes had already taken place, she reflected.

She had looked round her own rooms, which she had occupied since childhood, and had decided that she would make a special display in honour of the teddy bears and her brother's memory, but that it was definitely time to make a move to less girlish accommodation. She just wasn't the same person she had been a couple of months earlier.

Freed of fear, she had grown up all at once and, had the memory not now been so painful to her, she might have smiled when she recalled the absurdly juvenile outfit she had donned to run away on her wedding day. As it was, she had enjoyed installing herself and, of course, Edward the bear into a suite on the first floor of the villa. That had given her occupation and also the sense that she was making a fresh start within her own home.

Alexio had stayed on the island only until the will had been read. He had then flown to the Gakis headquarters in Athens to embark on the task of reorganising her father's holdings into a twenty-first-century business empire that would be open, accountable and efficient. Ione knew he was working eighteen-hour days and understood why he had made only a brief trip back for the funeral, but that did not ease her anxiety above the state of their marriage. It was now over a week since they had even kissed, never mind shared the same bed. Was this how it was all going to end? With Alexio just drifting further and further from her until finally she would have to face the fact that the man she loved no longer wished to be with her?

Yet never had Lexos looked more beautiful to her, Ione conceded ruefully. Against the backdrop of the glittering sunlit turquoise sea, the mountainous green slopes studded with the tall, arrow-shaped cypresses that seeded themselves naturally on the island looked breathtaking. She had not truly appreciated how much she loved Lexos until Kalliope had startled her with the news that she was leaving almost immediately to set up home in Athens.

'Your father liked me to live in his household and, of course, I was able to make myself useful here because your mother, Amanda, had no interest in domestic matters,' her aunt had pointed out with perfect truth. 'But I've always wanted to live in the city where I will be close to my friends. I know that my brother would not have approved but I am as excited as a girl about buying a first home of my own.'

For Ione, it had been an enlightening glimpse from another perspective of how restricted and empty Kalliope's life had been. Her aunt had never had the freedom that Ione herself had sought. The older woman had spent the greater part of her life running her brother's home and as that had been a role for which she had received little thanks, it was not surprising that the experience had soured her nature. Yet since Ione had abandoned her former rigid reserve with Kalliope, their relationship had improved and Ione had been embarrassed when her aunt had asked her permission to have friends visit her at the villa that afternoon.

Recognising that she ought to put in at least a brief appearance at that gathering, Ione suppressed a sigh and changed into a simple dark blue dress that nonetheless shrieked its Parisian origins and elegance. She had not even spoken to Alexio the day before and she felt rather too emotionally fragile for the challenge of making polite conversation. Indeed she was afraid the slightest thing would send her off into tears.

At about the same moment that Ione was treating her aunt's visitors to a welcoming smile, Alexio's helicopter was coming in to land on Lexos and a young man was coming up the steep drive to the villa after a long trudge up from the ferry docked at the harbour. An apprehensive expression on his thin, intelligent face, his jacket slung over one slim shoulder, the stranger paused to catch his breath.

Alexio was heading for the front entrance when he noticed him standing there and, with the natural courtesy that distinguished him in no matter what company he found himself, he approached him and introduced himself.

The young man said warily. 'My name is Yannis Kanavos. I…wondered if I could see Ione.'

Alexio froze in so much recoil from that declaration that he could not for an instant trust himself to speak. It was, he recognised, his worst nightmare come true at the very worst moment imaginable. The fisherman's son, Ione's one and only love, from whom she had been forcibly parted by her father. The rise of his own aggressive instincts was immediate.

'I see that you recognise my name.' Yannis stood his ground but he looked very young and apprehensive.

Kalliope had taken her visitors out to the loggia to admire the magnificent view but Ione had remained in the salon. As the door opened she glanced up. When she saw Yannis she could not believe her eyes and, without even realising it, she half rose from her seat. Her attention locked to the strained features of the young man whom she had known since childhood, she did not see Alexio enter in his wake. Indeed she was so much taken by surprise that only as Yannis spoke her name did she accept that it was truly him. Hurrying forward, she stretched out both hands for him to grasp.

'It *is* you—'

'Yes, it is I,' Yannis mumbled, as overcome with emotion as she was.

'Where have you been?' Ione whispered shakily, tears blurring her vision even as her face shone with happiness.

'I've been training with a medical relief team in Kosovo. I only heard of your marriage when I came home on leave.'

Entering the salon from the loggia, Kalliope Gakis recognised the unexpected visitor and the reunion taking place with an expression of unconcealed surprise and disapproval. She shot a startled look at Alexio and sped over to him to whisper, 'What is the Kanavos boy doing here?'

'He asked to see Ione.'

'And you allowed this?' Kalliope surveyed her niece's husband as though he had taken leave of his senses.

Alexio's sense of honour had triumphed over his more primal instincts. He had a very good idea of the courage it must have taken for Yannis to come to the Gakis home and he respected that, even if he wished him in hell, but what he was witnessing was no reward for his generosity: it was sheer punishment and torture. He had never seen Ione so relaxed and natural with anyone but himself, and certainly not with a man, but she had gone from joyful tears to laughter and was now engaged in deep conversation with her former boyfriend. Alexio stood there with his big hands clenched into controlling fists, painfully aware that Ione had not even noticed his arrival.

Only as Ione directed Yannis into a seat did she see

Alexio standing so straight and tall just inside the door. One glimpse of his lean, strong face was enough to make her heart leap, but the brooding darkness of his expression killed the delighted smile of relief that was ready to curve her lips.

'Alexio…' she said unevenly, wondering how long he had been there watching her making a fuss of Yannis, and feeling rather embarrassed and discomfited.

'I'm sure you and Dr Kanavos must have a lot to catch up on. I'll see you at dinner.' Alexio strode back out again, leaving her hovering in the centre of the room.

After Yannis had exchanged politer pleasantries with her uneasy aunt, Ione was keen to talk to him in private. 'Let's go for a walk,' she suggested and, responding to the older woman's scandalised appraisal with a soothing look, she left the room with Yannis.

They went straight down through the gardens, then towards the beach, for Yannis did not have long to spend on the island. With his usual independence, he had turned down her offer of a flight back to the mainland and he didn't want to miss the ferry, which only docked at Lexos for a couple of hours to offload supplies.

'Was it *your* decision to marry Alexio Christoulakis?' Yannis finally asked as they walked along the strand that would eventually wend round to the harbour. 'That's why I felt that I had to see you. I was afraid that your father had bullied you into the marriage.'

'I love Alexio,' Ione said simply.

Yannis smiled. 'I'm happy for you. I had already noticed that *he* loves *you* to bits!'

'Really?' Ione was dully amused by the confidence with which Yannis made that pronouncement.

'The minute Alexio realised who I was, he saw me as a threat. He didn't want to let me see you but he's a decent man. What have you been telling him about us to make him react that way? You were never in love with me,' Yannis reminded her with his sober smile. 'At most, we were loving friends. Isn't it strange how things can turn out for the best, only one doesn't see it that way at the time?'

Behind his father's back, Cosmas had helped the Kanavos family to make a fresh start on the mainland, but Yannis admitted that his parents would like to return to the island and Ione assured him that his family would be warmly welcomed home. Resolving to have their village home, which had been boarded up after their hurried departure, freshly decorated and aired in readiness, she watched Yannis depart on the ferry and then strolled back slowly and lost in her own thoughts to the villa.

Where Alexio was concerned, she *had* to stop hiding behind her pride, Ione acknowledged heavily. What true effort had she made to redress the damage that Kalliope's revelation had done to their marriage? How could she have believed that just telling Alexio that she would wait up for him a week ago was *any* kind of an olive branch? That had been an invitation to make love to her, to paper over the cracks with sex, she conceded in deep shame. It had been a shabby, superficial response to the situation and she could not blame him for reacting with contemptuous dismissal.

Wishing very much that God had allowed man to create a pair of binoculars that could see through hills to the harbour, Alexio was on his third stiff brandy by the time he saw Ione's tiny figure climbing the hill. His whole body leapt with relief. He had watched her walk away with Yannis and had not had a clue where she'd been going. He had gone through hell while he'd waited to find out. He had pictured her wandering hand in hand onto the ferry in some idyllic dream with Yannis. Letting her go had been the hardest thing he had ever done in his life, but he had done it only for *her* sake. But the instant Ione had been out of his sight, it had begun to seem like the craziest and stupidest thing he had ever done.

As Ione mounted the stairs Alexio was already striding across the vast galleried landing to greet her. 'You have come home…'

Wondering why he found it necessary to comment on the obvious, Ione collided with intense golden eyes and her ability to think straight vanished. She had to make a conscious effort not to just hurl herself at him as all the lonely, anxious insecurity of recent days welled up inside her.

'You're staying?' Alexio breathed hoarsely.

In silence, Ione nodded, beyond working out where he might imagine she could possibly have been going. He reached out a long-fingered hand and stroked his forefinger down her cheek in a curiously tender gesture before he let his lean fingers lace slowly into her hair. Her heart started thumping somewhere in the region of her throat, leaving her breathless. And then, in a sudden movement that shook her, Alexio hauled her up against him and brought his wide, sensual mouth down on hers with an explosive hunger that slivered through her like a flaming arrow hitting a target.

All the turmoil of the past week found release in the wild collision course of that fierce kiss. Lifting her off her feet, Alexio carried her across the sitting room where Edward the bear sat in innocent splendour and through to the bedroom beyond. She found herself on the bed sucking in oxygen even as Alexio came back down to her again, wrenching at his tie, throwing off his jacket, trying to do too many things at once but still a supreme success at continuing that kiss with the same fervour.

'Oh…' Ione gasped, excited to death and wholly delighted by his enthusiasm, but totally bemused.

'If you'd got on that ferry, I was going to follow you and tear the good doctor to pieces. I *couldn't* let you go…I just couldn't!' Alexio growled. 'Do you know what he said to me when I brought him indoors?'

'Er…no,' Ione mumbled, still striving to work that first reference to her getting on the ferry. He had believed she was about to run away with Yannis? Was he insane?

'Kanavos said that all that mattered to him was that you be happy and I could have happily killed the pious little jerk!' Alexio ground out with raw resentment. 'I want you to be happy too, but I want you to be happy only with *me*. I'm your husband. And if you're not happy with me, I want you to work at being happy. You don't belong with a guy like that. He wouldn't have any time for diamond-heeled shoes and teddy bears.'

'I know…Yannis is very serious and he would never run away with another man's wife. He also mentioned that he's on the brink of getting engaged to a nurse.'

Alexio gazed down at her with astonished dark golden eyes.

'I'm very fond of him. He was my brother's friend when we were children and I always liked talking to him, but even two years ago I knew I wasn't in *love* with Yannis,' Ione admitted ruefully. 'He's a special person and so good and kind but I was really just flirting with him—'

'Flirting…?' Alexio echoed thunderously.

'That's why I felt so dreadful when Papa assumed it was something more serious and had him thrown off the island. All that trouble because of me,' Ione sighed with deep regret.

With apparent difficulty, Alexio hinged his jaw shut again and breathed. 'And was he in love with you?'

'Infatuated, I think, at the start…but he felt we didn't have enough in common to even consider a future together.'

'I thought he'd come here to declare undying love in an effort to try and take you away from me!' Alexio launched down at her in condemnation.

'So you let me go all the way down to the ferry with him and thought I might not come back.' Comprehension had finally struck Ione and she surveyed him with shaken disbelief. 'What sort of a husband are you?'

A dark rise of blood accentuated Alexio's sculpted cheekbones.

Anger flared in Ione. 'I'm your wife. How could you think for one moment that I would take off with Yannis?'

'I wanted you to choose between us,' Alexio breathed tautly.

At that driven admission, Ione stilled in shock.

'You never made a free choice to be with me.' As her lush lips parted as though she intended to argue that point Alexio rested tormented golden eyes on her exquisite face. 'No, don't argue with me. Only answer one question. Did your father tell you you *had* to marry me?'

The silence thumped all around her while she attempted to find a way round that question but, if she was not prepared to lie, there was no way out. Her eyes stinging, Ione compressed her tremulous lips and she nodded in pained affirmation.

Alexio turned ashen pale beneath his olive skin. 'I should've known. So I was right. You had no choice and only after I tracked you down at the airport did you suddenly change your mind and decide to try and make a go of our marriage—'

'You're making things sound worse than they were—'

'No…there *is* nothing worse than finding out that you were *forced* into marrying me,' Alexio confided with a ragged edge to his dark, deep drawl.

Seeing the depth of his shock in his beautiful eyes and his instinctive recoil, Ione felt torn apart 'But—'

Alexio pressed his fingers against her lips to silence her. 'You were raised to be a dutiful Greek daughter. Yes, you originally planned to walk out on me. But when it started getting messy, when I confronted you…wasn't it easier for you just to make the best you could of our marriage?'

Ione was appalled when she finally grasped exactly what had been going through Alexio's mind over the previous nine days. He had worked it all out, put all the facts together to come up with a big picture that depicted her as a powerless victim throughout their entire relationship. 'No…it wasn't!' she argued with vehement conviction. 'In fact, it was one of the hardest things I ever did. As for being a dutiful daughter, at that point I didn't care. I'd spent *years* plotting, planning and dreaming about how I was going to trace my sister and build a new life. Then you got involved and all of a sudden I didn't know what I wanted any more. At the airport, all I could think about was *you* and how you would feel when you'd realised I'd gone. I wanted to be with you and that's the only reason I stayed…'

'Is that the truth?' Alexio's extraordinary eyes were pinned to hers with unashamed intensity.

'It doesn't matter how we started out…it only matters where we end up,' Ione whispered shakily. 'And I just want to end up with you. That's all. Nothing else. Just you.'

'I was so scared it would be Yannis,' Alexio conceded unsteadily, the strong bones of his face taut with tension.

'And I asked myself…how could I truly love you and yet stand in your way? How could I keep you with me when I already suspected that you had been forced into marrying me?'

How could I truly love you? A thousand butterflies were unleashed in Ione's tummy and she studied him with wondering fascination. 'I thought you buried your heart with Crystal…'

'My grief was real enough but it was based on guilt. I had to meet you before I understood that.' Alexio grimaced but candid golden eyes as rich as honey sought and held hers. 'By the time Crystal died, our engagement was on the skids, only I was too stubborn to accept that. I'd made a huge stand with my family over her and I didn't want to admit I'd made a mistake. That's not to say that I wasn't still very fond of her. We were together a long time—'

'You just didn't want to marry her any more,' Ione slotted in gently, her heart singing at his honesty. She knew what he wasn't saying: had his family not created such an outrageous fuss over his relationship with Crystal and challenged him, he might never have got engaged to her in the first place.

'I had to fall in love with you to understand that I'd never really been in love before, *agape mou*,' Alexio confided huskily. 'I cared more about you than I did about me. Pretty basic that, but that's the best definition.'

'And a very special one,' Ione whispered, tears catching at her throat.

'But I was devastated when I realised you'd booked a flight to leave me before we even got married because, while *you* were doing that, *I* was counting the days to our wedding! So finding out about that booking blew me away…I didn't know what to do…what to say. For the whole of the last week, I've been flailing around trying not to think about it and just burying myself in work—'

He loved her. He really, really loved her, but the more he bared his own emotions, the more she wanted to cry. 'You were so distant—'

'How do you act when you find out the woman you love was forced into marrying you? What do you say when you even understand why she did the things she did? I was very hurt...I felt like an idiot for not working it out for myself, but I didn't *want* to work it out,' Alexio admitted with an honesty that only made her tears flow faster and prompted him to tug her into his arms and hold her close while he smoothed her hair in an almost clumsy gesture because his hand wasn't steady. 'Once you told me the truth, I just felt like I had no right to *be* with you any more, no right even to think of you as my wife...because what choice had you had?'

'But I love you too,' Ione said in a wobbly voice. 'I love you so much. I was too scared to tell the truth in case I lost you—'

Alexio tilted her back from him and searched her swimming eyes with raw intensity. 'You love me too?'

Ione nodded.

'Then why are you crying?' Alexio demanded in bewilderment.

'I just felt *so* sad when I realised how miserable you'd been feeling all week—'

In a sudden manoeuvre, Alexio tipped her back against the pillows. 'Stuff the sad bit...are you just saying you love me because you feel sorry for me?'

'N-no,' Ione squeezed out with even greater difficulty. 'It's just that I spent all last week feeling more sorry for *me*—'

'You really love me?' Alexio still wasn't convinced.

'I'm crazy about you!' Ione gasped, irritation at his refusal to credit her declaration driving back the over-emotional tears as nothing else could have done.

A slashing grin transformed Alexio's lean, strong features. 'How crazy?'

'Can't live without you crazy…head over heels.' Happiness bubbling up inside her, Ione melted in the adoring appraisal her husband was giving her.

'There will never be another woman in my life, *agape mou*,' Alexio swore. 'I love you so much it hurts…'

He kissed her and she savoured the flood of hunger and love that enveloped her. It was pure bliss to know she was loved, to look into Alexio's tender gaze and know how important she was to him. The passion that followed as they struggled out of clothes and fell back into each other's arms with an extreme lack of cool was wild and stormy, for both of them needed to express that love and lie wrapped round each other afterwards, just revelling in the warmth of renewed intimacy.

'So…' Ione murmured, feeling wondrously relaxed and decidedly smug as she rested her appreciative but thoughtful gaze on Alexio's darkly handsome face, 'what about the…''what's mine is yours'' angle?'

Alexio tensed and then regarded her with considerable discomfiture. 'I couldn't stand for you to think that I would take advantage of you in any way. It was my pride talking…what little I had left after hearing Kalliope speak. I'm no fortune hunter—'

Ione studied him with a world of tender understanding in her gaze. 'I found my fortune in *you*,' she stressed. 'I need you as much as I need air to breathe.'

His breathtaking, teasing smile tugged at her heart-strings. 'I adore you…but give me five or ten years and I swear that *I'll* be keeping *you*!'

'I don't want you working such long hours that you're never with me!' Ione protested in dismay.

Laughing huskily, Alexio tumbled her down on top of him. 'When you're out of my sight for an hour, I miss you…*trust* me.'

And she did, she discovered with an instant lightening of her heart—she trusted him with every fibre of her being.

Eighteen months later, Ione spread an appreciative maternal appraisal between the pair of canopied cots in the nursery of the London townhouse.

Even three months after the birth of their twin son and daughter, her sense of achievement was still immense. Apollo had big brown eyes and dark curls and he slept like a log between feeds. Indeed Alexio had joked that their son only woke up to eat. Diantha was smaller and slept less and demanded much more attention. But each was utterly adored by their proud parents for the very different little personalities they were already beginning to display.

A wicked smile curved Ione's lips. She and her sisters had decided that it would be really great if they *all* had their children within a few years of each other so that their kids would fall into a similar age group. They had not thought it necessary to mention that ambition to their husbands. Freddy, of course, had had a headstart with little Ben and Karim, and had just recently given birth to a daughter, Azima, who was a perfect doll. Misty was eight months pregnant with a second son, who would be just great company for his brother, Connor. Ione had been delighted when she'd realised that she'd been carrying twins and to have a boy and a girl together had been the icing on the cake for her.

Not that Alexio had had that attitude. He had been really

worried when he'd realised that she'd been pregnant with two babies and she had got very tired during the last weeks, but there had been no complications during the birth. For Ione, it had been secretly wonderful just to have known that Misty and Freddy had been waiting outside the delivery room because Alexio had been so nervous that day he hadn't been able to hide it from her.

Her close relationship with her sisters was one of the greatest joys of Ione's once lonely life. She had met her father, Oliver Sargent, and, while she had found him charming company, she had been rather disappointed to feel no stronger bond, yet she had got on with his wife, Jenny, who was no relation at all, like a house on fire. But where her sisters were concerned, there had been no such disappointment. Freddy was so kind, Misty so full of life and fun, but both were equally loving and supportive. Mind you, it took Misty to throw her and Freddy for a loop, Ione conceded with a rueful smile of recollection...

Six months earlier, Alexio had thrown a fabulous surprise party for the twenty-fourth birthday his wife shared with her twin. That evening, Misty had arrived early with her arms tightly wrapped round a shabby cardboard shoebox and a look of uneasy strain on her vibrant face.

'I have a confession to make,' Misty confided guiltily to her sisters. 'There is one piece of information about our background that I've always held back from both of you. Our mother, Carrie, remarried when I was still a little kid. I couldn't make myself tell you that because it was just about the most hurtful thing I ever found out about her. All the time she'd been talking about how she was going to make a home for her and I and take me out of foster care, she was married to this guy who hadn't a clue I even existed!'

Feeling increasingly uneasy about withholding those

facts from her sisters, Misty had tried to make amends for her silence by discovering more information about their natural mother. It had been Freddy who had first learned when and where Carrie had died, but there had been a gap of quite a few years in their knowledge of how Carrie had lived between walking away from her twin daughters and her death alone in a city boarding house. Misty had traced their mother's landlady in the hope that she might remember Carrie. She had been shaken when the elderly woman had asked her to wait and had then reappeared clutching an old shoebox.

'It just seemed cruel to throw her keepsakes away and there was nobody to give it to for she never had any visitors. I always wondered who the kiddies in the photos were,' the older woman had explained.

Inside the box had been mementoes that had touched all their hearts and softened their attitude towards the woman who had brought them into the world, yet abandoned all three of them in turn. In worn envelopes they had found baby photos and locks of hair belonging to each of them. But the biggest surprise had been the revelation that there were *four* envelopes, not just three. And in the fourth envelope had been a lock of auburn hair and a colour snap of a tiny toddler with a shy, endearing smile that wrenched at their hearts, for they had known that that little girl must have been deserted by their mother just as they had been...

'I think we have another sister somewhere.' Misty was as usual the first to say out loud what Freddy and Ione were thinking. 'She might have been born during Carrie's second marriage but, as we don't know what her husband was called or anything at all about those years, we don't have a single lead to find her and I doubt if she even knows *we* exist! She may well be years younger...I mean,

Carrie was only in her early twenties when she had us...what if our little sister is in foster care all alone and with nobody?'

It could not be said that Alexio was overjoyed to be mopping up Ione's tears in the aftermath of all the worst-case scenarios Misty had come up with. Their husbands, Leone, Alexio and Jaspar too, swore that every effort would be made to find that little girl who had to be their sister. But there had been no trail to follow without establishing Carrie's whereabouts during those missing years and, so far, there had been no lucky breaks.

A powerful arm curved round Ione's slim shoulders, springing her back out of her rueful thoughts into the present. 'You're gloating over the twins again,' Alexio sighed in mock reproof.

'Why not? Being a mum is still so new to me.'

'You're a wonderful mother,' Alexio assured her.

Ione watched him studying his baby son and daughter with a pride and satisfaction that he could not hide and smiled. It did not occur to her even to mention that her thoughts had been on that fourth forlorn little sister in the photograph, for it would only remind Alexio that his efforts to discover a single fact that might lead them to her had been no more successful than that of her sisters' husbands.

And Ione, more than many women, knew just how lucky she was to have found real, lasting love with the man of her dreams. Every time Alexio looked at her she knew her feelings were equally matched by his. They spent a lot of their time based in the London townhouse that had once belonged to her brother. The decor had been rather outrageous when they'd first moved in and Alexio had been stunned by the spectacular swimming pool in the basement. Indeed the pool complex with its light displays, waterfall and mini-island could have starred on any film set. They had redecorated the rest of the house, and London, with the country house that they used on weekends, was their true home now.

The villa on Lexos was for holidays, the occasional business conference or for loaning out to Freddy and Jaspar or Misty and Leone for a romantic break because, love the island as she did, Ione found it rather too isolated after a couple of weeks. On the other hand it was the best possible place for her and her sisters and their families to get together because the house was so enormous. They also often entertained Alexio's parents and his sisters there. Ione had grown to love his family as much as her own and had a wonderful, warm relationship with her mother-in-law.

Alexio closed his hand over hers and tugged her out onto the landing, where he brought his mouth swooping down hungrily on hers with a roughened groan of satisfaction. 'Missed you today,' he muttered thickly before drowning out any possibility of a response with a second kiss.

'Missed Apollo and Diantha too…' The third kiss extracted a responsive moan from Ione's throat and Alexio took that as an invitation to sweep her up in his arms and carry her into their bedroom.

Alexio had had an evening meeting to attend, which he always hated, and Ione revelled in the comforting knowledge that he had been so keen to get home to her. But as he gazed down at her with possessive love in his eyes there was something about his smile, that oh, so sexy, wolfish smile of satisfaction, that etched a slight pleat between her brows.

'What happened today?' Ione asked.

'I'll tell you later…' Alexio's smile had a distinct tri-

umphal edge now, but as he followed it up by telling Ione
how gorgeous she was and taking off his shirt, an exercise
which always entranced her, she lost the plot at that stage.

'I adore you, Mrs Christoulakis,' Alexio murmured in-
dolently about an hour later, arms still tightly wrapped
around Ione. 'Don't ever think I don't appreciate you.'

In a dreamy-eyed state of blissful contentment, Ione felt
totally appreciated, indeed blessed.

'But sometimes I'm very selfish. I came home tonight
with news I couldn't wait to break and then I took one
look at you and I knew you'd be on the phone to Misty
and Freddy half the night…and I stalled,' Alexio completed with a grimace.

'Sorry?' As Alexio sat up Ione braced herself against
the pillows and looked at his darkly handsome features in
bewilderment, for she had not a clue what he was talking
about.

Alexio settled the phone helpfully on her lap. 'I've got
a lead that may hopefully help us to trace the *fourth*
Carlton sister…'

'Oh, my goodness!' Ione exclaimed, thrilled to death.
'What did you find out?'

As Ione grasped that Alexio had found out the surname
her natural mother must have used during her second marriage her green eyes brightened. Now that they had a name
to work with, it would surely only be a matter of time
until they traced their sister.

'I bet this annoys the hell out of Leone,' Alexio forecast.

'Why are men so competitive?' Ione reproved.

'And you're *not*?' Vibrant and amused golden eyes
raked over her. 'Then tell me how I know that next year
it'll be your turn to get pregnant again?'

Ione flushed. 'That's not being competitive.'

Alexio stretched like an indolent tiger and grinned.

'Don't worry about it, *agape mou*. Leone and Jaspar and I agreed that we quite enjoy the process.'

In the midst of dialling Misty's number, Ione gave him a mock punch in the ribs for that crack. He laughed and pulled her back into his arms. 'I love you,' he whispered huskily, sending a surge of happiness cascading through her, and on that particular night she didn't stay on the phone to either of her sisters quite as long as she might have done.

Modern Romance™
...seduction and
passion guaranteed

Tender Romance™
...love affairs that
last a lifetime

Sensual Romance™
...sassy, sexy and
seductive

Blaze
...sultry days and
steamy nights

Medical Romance™
...medical drama on
the pulse

Historical Romance™
...rich, vivid and
passionate

27 new titles every month.

*With all kinds of Romance for
every kind of mood...*

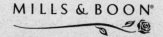

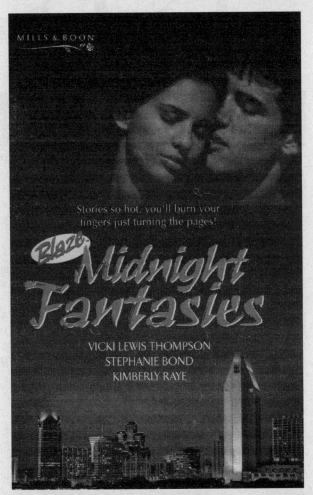

FREE

2 BOOKS
AND A SURPRISE GIFT!

We would like to take this opportunity to thank you for reading this Mills & Boon® book by offering you the chance to take TWO more specially selected titles from the Modern Romance™ series absolutely FREE! We're also making this offer to introduce you to the benefits of the Reader Service™—

★ FREE home delivery   ★ FREE gifts and competitions
★ FREE monthly Newsletter ★ Exclusive Reader Service discount
         ★ Books available before they're in the shops

Accepting these FREE books and gift places you under no obligation to buy; you may cancel at any time, even after receiving your free shipment. Simply complete your details below and return the entire page to the address below. *You don't even need a stamp!*

YES! Please send me 2 free Modern Romance™ books and a surprise gift. I understand that unless you hear from me, I will receive 4 superb new titles every month for just £2.55 each, postage and packing free. I am under no obligation to purchase any books and may cancel my subscription at any time. The free books and gift will be mine to keep in any case.

P2ZEC

Ms/Mrs/Miss/Mr ....Initials ....
                                                                        BLOCK CAPITALS PLEASE

Surname ....

Address ....

....

....Postcode ....

Send this whole page to:
UK: FREEPOST CN81, Croydon, CR9 3WZ
EIRE: PO Box 4546, Kilcock, County Kildare (stamp required)

Offer valid in UK and Eire only and not available to current Reader Service subscribers to this series. We reserve the right to refuse an application and applicants must be aged 18 years or over. Only one application per household. Terms and prices subject to change without notice. Offer expires 31st December 2002. As a result of this application, you may receive offers from other carefully selected companies. If you would prefer not to share in this opportunity please write to The Data Manager at the address above.

Mills & Boon® is a registered trademark owned by Harlequin Mills & Boon Limited.
Modern Romance™ is being used as a trademark.